THE LAST WOLF

by Gary Enright

THE LAST WOLF
The Legend of Three Toes

by Gary Enright

Published by:

> INSIGHT PUBLISHING DIVISION
> Insight Development Institute, Inc.
> 8130 Windwood Way
> Parker, CO 80134

Printed in the United States of America

Library of Congress Cataloging in Publication Data
Enright, Gary J.
The Last Wolf: The Legend of Three Toes/by Gary Enright
CIP 92-97035
ISBN 1-882159-65-9 $15.95 Softcover

ACKNOWLEDGEMENTS

Special recognition is due Kenneth Haraldsen, a native of Harding County, South Dakota who provided me with a treasure chest of information about the history of the wolf "Three Toes". Wally and Linda Stephens, owners and publishers of "Nation's Center News", Buffalo, SD assisted in obtaining historical documentation.

Dr. James Hutchinson, PhD, Executive Director of the Rocky Mountain Writers Guild receives my thanks for his frank and constructive evaluation of this work.

My thanks to those researchers, biologists and writers who have studied the lives, characteristics and science of wolves, from whose work I drew inspiration:

L. David Mech: The Way Of The Wolf, Voyager Press, and The Arctic Wolf: Living With The Pack National Geographic Society; Barry Lopez: Of Wolves And Men, Charles Scribner's Sons; Candae Savage: WOLVES: Text and Photographic Selection, Sierra Club Books; Sylvia A. Johnson and Alice Aamodt, WOLF PACK; Tracking Wolves In The Wild, Lerner Publications; and Diana Boyd of the "Wolf Ecology Project", Glacier National Park, University of Montana.

The cover of The Last Wolf is taken from a painting titled "Spirit Hunter", by artist Rick Kelley. Prints are available from Hudson Bay Fine Art Publishing, 18410 Priory Ave., Minnetonka, MN 55345.

Individual thanks go to Julie Johnmeyer, Kim Tatum, Kathy O'Brien and to my wife Felice Enright for their excellent editing work, and Kelli Dolecek for her word processing expertise.

And even though my father Thomas Enright has passed from our presence, he must be credited with the idea for this book, since he thrilled me with stories of the life of "Three Toes" during my childhood years.

My special thanks to you all.

Gary Enright

This book is dedicated to my wife Felice for all her hard work and her unending faith in me.

CHAPTER 1

Zando led the wolf family out of the Cave Hills heading toward the Little Missouri River.

Hunters had been pursuing the wolves for the past three days. They surprised them one morning as the wolves were returning to their rendezvous site after a night of hunting.

Each day the riflemen stalked them far into the night then set up camp on the trail when it became too dark to see.

Before sunrise, the hunters spread out looking for the wolf's tracks. When one of the riders saw sign of the wolves, he fired a shot to notify the others, and the hunt would begin again.

Zando was concerned about Laomi. She was expected to give birth to pups any day. He knew the constant running was hard on her, but she never complained.

"You need to stop and rest," Zando admonished his mate.

"Follow me," he indicated.

She obeyed.

Zando saw an area in the distance, covered with thick brush. It was an ideal place for Laomi to rest. He knew his mate was in danger of hurting herself or their unborn pups because she had to run continuously. She needed a place safe from the pursuing horsemen.

Zando led his mate to a chokecherry thicket.

"This will be good cover for us," he motioned as he found a small opening in the thick growth.

Zando instructed the remainder of the pack to continue on to the river.

"We'll stay here while you lead the hunters away," he motioned.

The wolves were careful not to leave their tracks close to the entrance as they continued their flight.

Zando warned Laomi, "Once we're inside we cannot escape if they see us."

Laomi did not reply.

Zando and Laomi lay close together. They could hear the hunters approaching a short distance away.

The wolves knew their pursuers did not have dogs with them and were certain they would not be discovered.

As they lay quietly, they watched the riders approach the thicket.

"There's a lot of tracks here," one of the riders shouted.

Another rode close to the bushes and dismounted. He examined the footprints, trying to determine the direction the wolves had taken.

"Looks like they all headed west," another observed.

Zando and Laomi lay motionless, blending into the drab background of the brush.

After circling the chokecherry bushes, the riders followed the trail left by the remaining pack members, and rode out of sight.

"We'll stay here and rest awhile," Zando indicated to his mate.

Laomi agreed.

Farther west, the rest of the wolves were led by Skola, the oldest son of Zando and Laomi. He guided the pack across the river, into the heavy timber and brush on the west side. There he instructed the family to find hiding places and wait for Zando and Laomi, the alpha male and female.

After a few hours, Acalya, a young female of the pack, led some of the others to the river to drink.

"Keep a watch for the hunters," Skola cautioned.

Acayla nodded her understanding.

After drinking, she and another young female began to explore the edges of the river bank.

They were not searching for anything in particular, simply satisfying their curiosity about the area since they had never been here before.

Suddenly Acalya heard the beat of horses' hooves. The sound was close.

Acalya panicked.

"I hear horses and riders," she communicated to her companion.

"We must get away from the river and find a place to hide."

Acalya searched frantically for logs or a pile of brush to hide in, but saw nothing.

Then as the sound of the riders grew louder, Acayla saw a small indentation in the river bank.

"Quick," she admonished, "We'll hide here."

The wolves entered the opening and were surprised to find that it was a small cave stretching several feet back under the river bank.

The pair moved into the darkness of the cavity, disappearing from sight just as the riders reached the opposite bank of the river.

"I don't see any sign of the varmints," a rider announced.

"They probably took off into the timber west of here," another commented.

We'd better turn back, the sky looks bad," a third rancher stated.

"Yeah," the last of the group agreed, "Looks like it might snow."

The riders sat astride their horses for a few minutes, talking about the darkening sky.

"We should get on home before it starts snowing," the first cowboy declared.

They agreed, turned their horses eastward and rode away from the river.

Acalya slowly crept toward the den entrance and watched the riders depart.

Still uneasy about nearly being discovered, the two young females stayed inside the cave until they were certain the horsemen had left.

Meanwhile, Zando and Laomi crawled out of the chokecherry thicket and continued toward the river and their family.

"We must be cautious," Zando communicated to Laomi.

The two wolves wisely followed the hoof prints of the horses which pursued the tracks of the rest of the pack.

As the two approached the river, Laomi cautioned Zando, "I hear horses."

Zando stopped and crouched beside his mate. The pair listened intently.

After a few minutes, Zando crawled to the top of a ridge and looked down into the valley leading to the river.

"The hunters are leaving," he signaled Laomi.

She quickly moved to his side to watch the retreating riders.

As Zando watched the hunters ride away, Laomi observed two young wolves in the distance, along the river bank.

"There's Acayla," Laomi indicated.

Zando focused on the river. "Everything seems to be alright," he motioned.

"I'm sure it is," Laomi responded.

Then she added, "Everyone must be safe since we did not hear shots."

When the riders disappeared into the distance, Zando and Laomi trotted toward the river.

As they moved through the rugged hills, Zando noticed that an uneasy calm had spread across the prairie.

Everything was silent.

Laomi was the first to reach the river bank. She was met by Acayla who nuzzled her affectionately.

"We were worried about you," the younger female indicated to Laomi.

"Zando and I hid in some bushes," she indicated.

"I'm glad you're safe," Acayla motioned.

"I have something to show you," Acayla continued.

The younger wolf led her pregnant friend to the entrance of the small cave she and her companion had just discovered.

"This will be a perfect den for the pups," she signaled excitedly.

"I agree," Laomi responded.

While the females investigated the new den, Zando crossed the river and began searching for Skola and the rest of his family.

He found them hiding in the heavy trees about a mile from the river.

"The hunters have left," he indicated to the pack.

The leader then signaled the wolves to follow him back to the river.

As they approached the river bank, he saw Laomi and Acayla emerging from the dugout.

He observed a half dozen huge cottonwood trees above the well-hidden entrance.

Laomi approached her mate and excitedly announced, "Acayla has found a perfect den."

He entered the structure.

"It's exactly what we need," he signaled.

As he emerged from the newly found den, he looked toward the sky.

A gigantic cloud bank rose in the northwest and soon covered the horizon. Everything turned gray. Even the pine covered hills disappeared into a heavy fog as a late spring blizzard approached.

The temperature fell rapidly. The balmy spring day suddenly turned bitter cold. In minutes it was below freezing.

Wind whistled down the winding river, announcing the oncoming snow.

As alpha male of the pack, Zando, knew it was his responsibility to help his mate prepare the whelping den.

Laomi became more anxious as the impending birth approached. She was easily irritated and tolerated Zando's help only to the point of allowing him to enter the passageway to dig it clear of debris.

With the storm rapidly approaching, every member of the pack helped.

Some of the wolves went in search of game. Since the hunters had pursued the wolf family for three straight days, there had been little opportunity to eat.

Laomi was busy preparing the interior. Flood waters had deposited soft river sand in the den and Laomi scratched the substance into small mounds.

She dug a bed for herself with her forepaws, then rearranged the mounds of sand with her muzzle.

The snow was beginning to fall. She hoped the opening to the den would be high enough to remain above the spring floods which were sure to come after the late season storm.

Laomi growled fiercely at her mate as he tried to enter the den itself. She knew her time was near.

Sensing this and respecting her need for privacy, Zando withdrew. Then, as if to save face, he growled at the other wolves on his way out, warning them to keep their distance.

Five of the wolves that left to go hunting brought down a crippled doe. They carried several pieces of venison back to the river for Laomi and those who remained to prepare the den.

The storm was building.

The wind swirled the snowflakes into a blinding mass so thick the animals could barely see one another.

Each wolf searched for shelter.

The blizzard caught many of the animals off guard.

Ravens, the wolves hunting companions, flew into the timber to wait out the storm.

Field mice, already preparing their nests, burrowed into their underground shelters.

Rabbits, which earlier in the day had been playfully looking for fresh new grass for their diets, scurried to their holes, secure from the danger of becoming victims of the snow, or of hungry wolves.

Rapidly falling temperatures created a thin layer of ice over the water, making crossing hazardous.

Nevertheless, the pack found shelter on both sides of the river, all within view of the den where Laomi was about to give birth.

Zando settled into a small dugout on the hillside just across the river.

He could barely see the entrance to the den through the thick blowing snow. Yet he knew Laomi would be safe from danger and secure in the den.

Years of experience as the leader gave him an added sense of awareness.

Zando knew wolves had no real enemies except man and starvation.

For this brief period during the blizzard, he would be able to relax his guard against man. They were not likely to be out in a raging storm.

As he lay watching the storm enclose the countryside, he had visions of generations past which fought to defend the right of wolves to exist.

Zando was descended from a long line of leaders. His ancestors lived in this region centuries before the white man came with his wagons, cattle and sheep.

The wolves coexisted in relative peace with the only other humans they knew, the plains Indians.

There was a spiritual relationship between wolves and Indians.   This kinship involved mutual respect and admiration. It was known as *nature's spirit*.

Indians admired the wolves for their craftiness, stealth and hunting abilities.

The wolf regarded the Indian as a useful neighbor, one who often left a food supply after a successful hunt.

Occasionally, wolves became victim to the Indian. They were sometimes killed for ceremonial purposes. The hide and head were used by medicine men in their healing and hunting rituals.

Wolves maintained a cautious respect for all men and purposely avoided them whenever possible.

Families of wolves lived on this continent centuries before the Indian's ancestors crossed that small strip of land connecting the two great land masses in the frozen lands of the north.

The wolves accepted the intruders because these people held a similar relationship with nature, the Great Mother of the earth.

Zando had an instinctive knowledge of this ancestral coexistence. These brothers of the plains lived from the land, taking only what was necessary to survive.

Indians respected wolves because they performed a service to nature by removing diseased and weak animals from the herds of deer, elk, buffalo, and pronghorn.

Wolves and Indians shared similar traits including the creation of territories. Just as the Indians defended their hunting grounds against other tribes, wolves guarded their domain against the intrusion of other packs.

They shared the same game and worked jointly in an unspoken agreement to preserve nature's balance.

Zando was now about to pass these instincts and remembrances of past generations on to his offspring being born in the den a few yards away.

Zando had a reputation as a fierce fighter; he was quick, smart and cunning. He was now eight years old. He had been the pack's leader for five years, following in his father's, grandfather's, and great-grandfather's paths.

As the direct descendant of generations of wolf leaders, it was his duty to train his successor for leadership.

He understood his responsibility to protect those which had been placed in his care.

He lay looking down on the other wolves in the pack. Several were his sons and daughters, but of the males, none displayed qualities he desired in his successor.

Two years ago Zando had high hopes for his son Cular. The young wolf had shown great promise. However he was viciously killed by hunters.

The younger wolf exposed himself to riflemen while leading other young wolves to safety. The promising leader was gone.

It was during this massive hunt by ranchers that more than half of the pack was killed or driven from the region. The constant hunting pressure drove wild game away and made food supplies scarce. For the first time in many years, some of the pack starved.

Zando and Laomi developed a dread and hatred for the white man and his weapons. These instinctive emotions were passed on to each of their young along with their intense courage to defend their territory.

Zando led his family through some very difficult years. But now, time was against him. He needed a strong, intelligent heir to succeed him.

There was something different about the circumstances surrounding the birth of this batch of pups.

Zando did not fully understand, but he believed in the force the Indians referred to as the Great Spirit. He believed that this spirit lived among the animals as well as among men. He had felt its presence many times.

Now he was aware of this power surrounding the pack as the time for Laomi to deliver her pups approached.

Laomi had indicated that these unborn pups were unusually active. Often Zando was awakened at night by Laomi's whines and barks as the pups kicked inside her belly.

Even their mating for this litter was extraordinary. They mated in February, the month of the Snow Moon.

Laomi was very aggressive and saw to it that Zando stayed away from the other female wolves who were also in heat.

The pair-bonding between Zando and Laomi was continuous, and they constantly showed affection for one another. But now it intensified.

She wanted him to breed her before any of the other females had an opportunity to entice him. Something beyond the natural urging of her annual breeding cycle commanded Laomi to become pregnant and bear Zando's pups this year.

Laomi snarled and bit the other males of the pack when they made advances toward her and she did the same to the females as they approached Zando.

She was successful.

Now, during this mating period, the two wolves spent many days together, playing and enjoying one another, rekindling their affection.

On a cold clear night when the moon reached its fullness, they mated.

Zando's thoughts drifted back to the time when they first mated five years before. Laomi had changed very little since then. Her coat was a beautiful cream color. Her shoulders had darker pelage hairs and her white muzzle was flecked with brown and black whiskers. Her chest and underbelly were pure white and her legs were light tan.

Laomi was quiet and aloof. Her dignified posture added to her credibility as the alpha female.

Now Zando lay silently in the dugout, his face buried under the long hair of his rear legs and tail. Snow piled up around him.

He could no longer see the river because of the blinding storm, but he knew Laomi was giving birth to their pups.

He believed she would fulfill his longing for a son to carry on his family's dynasty.

CHAPTER 2

Laomi paced in a tight circle inside the den. Her piercing eyes surveyed every detail of the enclosure, even though the cave was pitch black.

The den was an exceptionally good find. In past years, Laomi had given birth to pups in a variety of shelters. This den, however, was roomier and better hidden.

The den's interior was plain, no bedding, just a floor of packed river sand under the ancient trees. The huge root system provided support overhead and held the walls of the structure in place.

It was apparent the den had been hollowed out by swirling flood waters many years before. A variety of animals had used the facility but it was abandoned when Acayla located it.

Acayla was a one-year-old female. She was smart and mature for her age, a prime candidate to become the alpha female, to share leadership with an alpha male.

Even though she was subservient to Laomi and Zando, Acayla was Laomi's closest female companion and obvious successor.   Laomi spent hours training Acayla in the strategies of hunting.

The youngster was adopted by the pack after she was found abandoned near a den of another pack. Their den had been raided by hunters who killed all the pups except her.

When the attack came on her family, Acayla hid quietly in the sagebrush where she had been playing.

This night, Laomi knew that Acayla was keeping watch over the den entrance. She could hear the wind whistling as she ended her pacing and settled down to endure the labor pains now only minutes apart.

As she awaited the birth of her pups, Laomi remembered how she was chosen by Zando.

She was three years old at the time. Her family structure was well established. Her father and mother were the alpha male and alpha female of their pack. They dominated a large territory in the foothills of the Big Horn Mountains.

Laomi was one of three pups.

Her sister Beska had been killed by hunters when she was a year old. Her brother Targar reacted strongly to their sister's death and became increasingly unruly.

The despondent wolf picked fights with other members of the pack and was impatient and rough with the pups and yearlings.

Increasingly, Targar gained a reputation as a renegade. His constant attacks on livestock, belonging to the ranchers who had killed his sister, brought the hunters out in force against the pack.

He was finally driven from the family by their father to maintain order in the pack. This was necessary to avoid challenges to the leadership and to stop treacherous treatment of other family members.

Laomi was saddened by Targar's departure and sensed she would never see him again.

With her only sister dead and her brother gone, she felt totally alone.

Her preoccupation with these thoughts was interrupted the day Zando boldly entered her pack's territory. He was the handsomest male she had ever seen.

There was an aura about him which immediately attracted her.

Laomi was impressed by Zando's color. His coat was nearly black, with flecks of gray. His muzzle and legs were gray and his tail was thick and bushy.

His body was fuller than most wolves she had known. His strong shoulders revealed his strength.

Through his gestures, Laomi's family knew he had come to select a mate. He studied the younger members of the opposite sex.

Several males snarled and were hostile toward Zando, but oddly, none were courageous enough to attack.

Laomi saw that Zando had the appearance of a leader, yet he was careful to show deference to her father, respecting his position as alpha male.

Laomi's father stood erect, tail high in the air, while Zando moved closer to the pack with his tail slightly elevated. He was not challenging her father's position, but still sent a clear message that he was a dominant wolf.

It took a great deal of courage for a single wolf to enter another pack's territory and approach them alone.

A lesser wolf, without such grace and audacity, would have been attacked and driven off or killed.

In his dignified way, Zando paid respect to the alpha male and female yet watched the other members of the pack as he proceeded to make his intentions known.

Laomi withdrew to the edge of a small grove of trees as Zando approached her. She watched him carefully.

When Zando reached Laomi, she lowered her head and she rolled over on her back in submission. She licked his face as he stood over her, growling.

It was not the fierce growl of attack, but the signal of dominance, common among wolves.

Immediately upon Laomi's acquiescence, the atmosphere of hostility in the pack ended. The two wolves mutually made the choice to be mates. The other wolves had no input into the matter. Their union would not be challenged, none objected to Laomi leaving with this visiting wolf.

Zando signaled Laomi's father, "I have no intention of staying. My family lives far to the east of here and I must return."

Zando had fulfilled his intention of obtaining a mate that would be the mother of his offspring, thus providing for new blood for his pack. He knew the generations to come would need strength, proficiency, and intelligence to survive.

Zando and Laomi left immediately to return to his territory.

As they traveled, Zando communicated his strong feelings about carrying out the purposes of *nature's spirit*.

During the trip, Laomi learned much from Zando about the purpose wolves play in nature.

"I have always had these thoughts," she communicated to him.

"Together we will build a strong, intelligent family and restore our rightful place in creation," Zando relayed.

As the couple traveled, Laomi stayed close to Zando's side. They shared everything. Laomi used her skill in maneuvering game into ambush, and Zando used his speed and strength to run down the animal they selected.

It took them five days to travel the distance from Laomi's home to the Slim Buttes where Zando's family lived.

Laomi remembered how restless she was the night before they reached Zando's home.

"I am anxious to know your family and become acquainted with this new territory," she proclaimed.

She knew it would be different than her life in the mountains. Hunting on the prairie was a new experience.

The excitement of these new surroundings peaked her senses, and she anticipated her future responsibilities.

Laomi realized she must learn the terrain, the habits of the game and the different talents of the members of the pack.

When they arrived, both were welcomed by Zando's family.

Zando's parents, the alpha male and female, warmly greeted Zando, but Laomi was forced to submit to the older wolves' authority.

They all observed her carefully, testing her to determine her place in the pack.

Laomi did not feel any hostility. It was as if she had always known this family. She was determined to work hard for their acceptance.

It was clear that Zando's parents were preparing him for leadership.

While they maintained their positions, Zando's father often conferred with his oldest son in many decisions. Laomi also found her relationship with Zando's mother to be exceptionally close.

There was no doubt in Laomi's mind that Zando's parents were relieved that their son had found a suitable mate and the role of leadership would soon be passed on.

The changes came more rapidly than anyone expected.

Within a few weeks of their return, Zando and Laomi were established as the alpha male and female. Tragically, Zando's father and mother were both killed the same day.

Zando's mother had been caught in a trap. His father stayed close by her throughout the night, refusing to leave her side.

Early the next morning, the trappers spotted both wolves from a distance and shot them.

The impact of losing both parents struck Zando hard. His immediate reaction was to strike back, but his intelligence was too great to yield to such foolishness. If he reacted unwisely, the whole pack would be in jeopardy.

The transition of authority came naturally. The pack quickly accepted Zando and Laomi's leadership.

Laomi's strong personality enabled her to assume the role of alpha female without creating animosity among the other females.

Even though she was a newcomer, she had earned everyone's respect. She gained status by being Zando's mate, but she increased her importance by displaying hunting abilities exceeding those of any other member.

Laomi was now in her fifth year as alpha female. Over the years she had become an important leader, bearing strong, healthy pups, teaching them her skills and sharing command with her mate.

Now Laomi rested between labor pains.

She sensed the weather outside had worsened. She thought about Zando and whether he was sheltered from the storm.

Since becoming Zando's mate, Laomi had given birth to four batches of pups. This pregnancy, however, had been the most unusual of them all.

Several strange things occurred, including her strong compulsion to mate with Zando earlier that spring. She understood the natural order of things, but she did not fully understand the strong sense of urgency she felt during the mating season.

As she awaited the impending birth of the pups from that mating, her thoughts turned to the strange reunion she had with her brother Targar.

During the past winter, Laomi thought she recognized Targar's scent along the trails at the edge of their territory. But the years had faded her familiarity with his essence and she believed her mind could be playing tricks on her.

It may have been her desire to see him alive that overpowered her ability to distinguish between various wolf scents.

Laomi had not seen her brother since he left the family. He had lived a solitary life, encroaching on the territories of many different wolf packs.

He had traveled eastward during these years, finally arriving in Zando and Laomi's territory.

That was six weeks ago, shortly after Laomi had become pregnant with this batch of pups.

There was an irony in their last meeting, one which Laomi would remember her entire life.

Targar approached their pack.

Zando, ever protective of his family and territory, warned, "Keep your distance."

Targar continued to approach cautiously, ignoring Zando's warning to stay out of their domain.

Laomi recognized the intruder and trotted to the edge of the pack's protective security.

"It's my brother Targar," she exclaimed.

She and her brother stood fifty yards apart, staring at one another.

Laomi motioned for Targar to come closer, but the wolf stood at a distance without moving.

Zando, having never met Targar, was apprehensive, but sensed that this wolf meant something special to Laomi.

Without a sound, Laomi and Targar communicated messages of hello and farewell.

Laomi wanted to rush to her brother's side, but an unseen power prevented her from doing so.

After a few minutes, Targar turned and ran to a hill a quarter mile away. He stood there, looking back at his sister one last time.

Then he raised his head and looked away.

Zando came to Laomi's side, watching the lone wolf.

Then they both looked in the direction Targar faced and saw riders coming towards them.

The hunters spotted Targar and began to ride rapidly toward the lone wolf on the hill.

Targar turned and ran away from Laomi and her pack, leading the riflemen in the opposite direction.

Laomi and her mate signaled the family to be quiet and to hide in the brush nearby. They watched as the hunters pursued Targar over the distant hills. It was obvious that he had purposely distracted them.

Since that day, no member of the pack reported seeing Targar again.

Laomi was convinced that he gave his life to save her and her unborn pups.

Now this extraordinary pregnancy was about to end.

As the weather outside worsened, Laomi began her hours of giving birth.

CHAPTER 3

It was a stressful labor.

Hours passed before the final contractions became one long painful agony.

The first pup reluctantly emerged from the birth canal.

He was the largest pup Laomi had ever given birth to. The three others that followed came easily with periods of rest in between.

When a pup emerged, the doting mother began to lick it to help the drying process. She didn't want the cooler temperatures outside to create a fatal chill in the newborn.

They were all very active, finally free of the confinement of the womb.

Instinctively all four pups moved to her mammaries, filled with rich mother's milk.

The pups were unable to see or hear and were nearly helpless. Laomi nudged them toward her breasts since they could not yet move on their wobbly legs.

Laomi curled up so her newborn were nestled in the warmth of her stomach. Her front and rear legs formed a barrier to the chilly air of the den.

The female rested as she watched the pups eat their first meal. While they sucked, she napped. It had been a long night.

Experience taught her that for a few days, the pups would be helpless and she could rest.

As the first night passed, Laomi licked each pup again and again. The two males and two females awoke periodically, grunting softly, looking for the nourishment of their mother's warm milk.

Early the next morning, Zando appeared at the den entrance. Laomi arose from her lying position to greet him with a warning growl.

This was her protective instinct for the pups, but it also communicated that everything was fine. It would be several days before she would allow him to view his children.

Later that day, Acayla came to the den entrance. Laomi greeted her with the same warning. The visit was brief. Only a friend making sure everything was okay.

Zando deposited pieces of venison at the den entrance. Laomi ate the food as quickly as Zando moved away. The hungry pups created a tremendous appetite in the mother.

Spring blizzards were not uncommon and normally Zando would not have been concerned. However, the birth of this family of pups caused him anxiety. This was an important event and he worried that something might go wrong.

Zando considered the dangers.

If the strong winds continue to pile the snow into drifts, the entrance to the den may be blocked. Laomi and the pups could suffocate, he thought.

He also considered the hazards of hunters.

"After the blizzard stops, they can easily follow our tracks to the den and kill the newborn pups," he pondered.

At the end of the second day, snow had drifted over the den entrance. Zando spent most of the evening clearing the opening, while the high winds continued to swirl the snow around him.

Laomi and the pups needed fresh air and food. He supplied both.

The sun rose over the wolf family's home on the third morning. The storm was over.

Already the largest of the four pups was romping inside the den, bumping into his mother and the smaller pups.

Laomi had to get up to retrieve the pup who was already exploring the entrance tunnel of the den, even though his eyes were not yet open.

He was the most active and lively pup she had ever seen, especially at this age.

Acayla came to the den entrance carrying food for Laomi.

Laomi allowed her to come into the den far enough to see the four pups.

Then Laomi growled, warning Acayla, "That's close enough for now."

After a few moments, Acayla dropped the food, backed out and left.

Later that afternoon, Laomi came to the entrance of the den. She was thirsty. She took huge bites of snow near the den entrance and surveyed the white kingdom outside.

Zando watched his mate as she relieved herself and again entered the enclosure.

Each day Laomi came out of the den to eat the food which was deposited by Zando and other members of the pack. The cache of deer meat was now covered by the deep drifts and the wolves knew it was time to hunt.

Zando instructed Skola, the beta male, to take a few members of the family and find fresh meat.

They left early that evening in search of deer which occupied the territory.

"There are deer foraging in a small valley along the creek," Skola motioned to his companions.

The wolves discovered the deer were completely surrounded by deep drifts.

"Nature has helped us," one of the younger wolves observed.

Several of the deer were weakened by the storm since most of the grass was covered by the deep snow. Some of the older deer were thin and they lacked the strength to survive much longer.

Skola motioned toward the weaker deer, selecting these animals as their target.

Circling, the wolves made the deer nervous. Finally, the deer broke through the drifts to freedom.

The older and weaker deer soon fell behind in the escape. One of these became nourishment for the wolf pack.

The wolves ate heartily.

"We must take food back to the den for Laomi and the others," Skola instructed his hunting comrades.

They returned to the den with a supply of food for those who did not go on the hunt.

Each was greeted on their return by the others who rushed to them, licking and nipping at their mouths until the hunters regurgitated some of the contents of their stomachs.

Everyone ate their fill.

Laomi had fresh meat to help her regain her strength.

The hunting wolves returned to the carcass and tore large pieces of venison off and carried it back to be cached near the den.

Within a week, the snow had started to melt in the warm spring sunshine. Laomi appeared at the entrance to the den to enjoy the spring day.

The river was beginning to run rapidly with the runoff from the nearby hills.

Zando approached, but stopped a few feet away when he saw the hairs raise on the back of her neck. He knew her protective message. "Do not come too close."

The two wolves moved their heads in unison and the fur on Laomi's neck lay back down. Zando approached her, nuzzling her mouth and licking her face.

He missed being next to his mate and touching her as he had for years.

Nervously Laomi kept a constant eye on the pups curled up in the soft sand just inside the den entrance.

The April sun felt warm and pleasant to the new mother.

In a few days much of the snow disappeared.

The alpha female enjoyed being outside the den, rejoining the other wolves.

The pack relished the spring weather by spending their days hunting and playing.

Fortunately, the ranchers were busy with their cattle and sheep and were not taking time to hunt the wolf pack. Because of the abundance of deer weakened by the spring blizzard, the wolves had ignored the young calves and lambs.

The wolves harvested numerous feasts from the wildlife which had become storm victims.

Inside the den, Laomi was well fed by Zando and Acayla who visited her daily with fresh meat.

The pups were now two weeks old and ready to come outside for the first time.

Zando approached Laomi at the den entrance.

"It's time to bring them out," she indicated.

The alpha male quickly signaled to his mate that she should wait until he checked for danger.

Zando emerged from the den and scouted the nearby vicinity.

When he was satisfied that it was safe, Zando entered the den passageway and signaled Laomi.

Curious to see the new pups, all the wolves gathered near the den entrance when Laomi appeared, leading the furry babies.

The pups were playful and alert, but it was their first time in daylight and their sensitive eyes caused them to be shy and uncertain.

Laomi nudged each pup outside with her nose, pushing them into an unfamiliar world, encouraging them to be brave.

"It's okay," she indicated, "This is your family."

Acayla approached first, nuzzling each pup under the watchful eye of Laomi.

Zando waited and observed. After each member of the pack family approached the pups, making their acquaintance, he took his turn.

"Come and meet your offspring," Laomi signaled to Zando. She could see his pride and her look of affection toward him was unmistakable.

He approached cautiously, touching noses with Laomi first, then sniffing each pup as they stood tentatively under their mother's belly.

To the pups, Zando was an awesome sight. His stately posture intimidated the little ones, but they recognized he was someone special in their lives, and sensed his authority.

The largest pup was the first to approach his father.

Bravely stepping away from his brother and sisters, this pup distanced himself from the protection of his mother. He moved close to Zando's outstretched nose. Zando laid down in front of the youngster.

The young pup put his paws on his father's face and started licking Zando's muzzle.

Zando gently licked the pup, nearly knocking him over with his powerful tongue.

Those first moments created a bond between father and son. Laomi watched proudly, sensing the importance of this time being shared by the two.

Within minutes, all the pups lost their initial fear. They felt safe and protected with their new family.

They ventured down the small incline at the front of the den.

They looked at everything, jumping at the slightest movement or sound, scurrying back to the safety of their mothers side when they felt the least bit threatened.

Zando stood proudly watching the exploration.

He carefully evaluated each pup. They were healthy and strong.

One stood out from the others.

He was more alert.

He stood erect and took his steps deliberately.

He was the firstborn.

He was larger and stronger than the others.

It would be difficult for Zando not to play favorites. For some reason he had a special attraction to this pup. He was proud of each of his offspring, but this one was different.

He was anxious to start teaching all the youngsters. Then he could determine each of their talents, instincts and knowledge.

But that would have to wait until they matured. For now he and Laomi would simply enjoy the playful bundles of fur.

Teaching would come later.

CHAPTER 4

Wolves have a clearly defined social order. It exists at all age levels. At four weeks of age, the pups began learning where they fit into the family.

Even before they were weaned, the pups started to learn which of their siblings were dominant.

Later, they would be taught the rank of each member of the pack. Instinctively wolves know that no matter what their status, each must be in command of their own actions. Wolves accept their rank since each tier is important to the overall survival of the pack. They have learned over the centuries to preserve their individuality and self worth.

Zando and Laomi paid close attention to these pups recognizing the unusual events leading up to their birth. They especially watched the larger one.

They communicated to the other wolves that this youngster would be known by the Lakota Indian name Wakan, meaning mystery.

He had a dark gray coat. His face was highlighted with light gray hairs on each cheek and around the eyes and heavy black over the forehead and around the ears.

Wakan was the first to show the instincts of a hunter.

Whenever members of the pack brought meat for Laomi, Wakan would attack it, tearing at it with his milk teeth and wrestling with the larger pieces.

Soon, the other pups followed his example.

Later, when Zando brought bones to the den for his family, Wakan pounced on them, growling fiercely.

Acayla and the other wolves brought pieces of deer hide for the pups. Laomi taught them how to play tug-of-war in order to help strengthen their jaws and develop strong teeth.

As the weather warmed and the spring sunshine dried the sand along the riverbank, Laomi took the pups outside every day.

During these outings, they became better acquainted with their father and the rest of the pack.

Acayla was enchanted with Wakan. She followed him whenever he ventured more than a few feet away from his mother.

Acayla encouraged the pup's natural curiosity by letting him explore on his own.

Wakan loved to roll in the sand and jump off the low clay mounds along the river.

Often, in his enthusiasm, he tumbled into shallow pools along the water's edge. Acayla or his mother were always nearby to come to his rescue, although it was seldom necessary. Usually he jumped up and continued his games.

The afternoon was their favorite time. Basking in the warm sunshine, Laomi watched the other members of the pack play with the pups and began to teach the first lessons in stalking.

They did this by hiding small bits of meat for the pups to find. This exercise developed their sense of smell and direction.

When Wakan was just six weeks old, he proudly returned to his mother's side with a live mouse in his mouth.

"Look what I caught," he indicated, proudly showing off his catch.

Laomi had watched her son capture the rodent in the nearby grass.

She was pleased that he spent several minutes stalking his prey, then pounced on it as it tried to escape.

"I'm proud of you," Laomi expressed as she licked the fur on the top of Wakan's head.

The other three pups rushed toward Wakan, curious to see why he was receiving so much of their mother's attention.

In the confusion, the mouse escaped momentarily, but Wakan quickly recovered the tiny animal. This time however, the mouse was agitated and defended himself by biting Wakan on the lip.

Surprised and confused, the youngster dropped the mouse and rushed to the safety of his mother's side.

Laomi licked the pup's mouth to sooth his injury. Then, realizing he wasn't badly injured, Wakan quickly ran after the mouse again.

The mouse escaped in the tangle of pups, each stumbling over the other in an attempt to capture Wakan's prize.

It was during this playful time of learning that each pup developed individuality. There was an immense difference in their personalities and each would play a definite part in the daily routine of the pack's life.

Within weeks, each pup received a name.

The larger of the two females, was named Sapa, the Lakota Indian word for black, because of her extremely dark fur. Strongly resembling her father's coloring, Sapa was aggressive and playful.

Ohake, the smaller female, received the Lakota name for mixed gray color. Her personality was quiet and reserved.

And Nehma, Wakan's smaller brother, was named because of his quiet, secretive manner.

It was not uncommon to find these names among the plains wolves since their ancestors had lived for centuries among the Indians.

Before the white man came, wolves trusted the Indians to come into their living areas. At times the Indian children played with the wolf pups but caused them no harm. This forged a bond between Indians and wolves that passed through hundreds of generations.

But this was no longer true since the Indians were gone and the white man had shown himself to be the wolves' enemy.

The four pups were weaned, at about two months of age. Members of the pack took turns playing with them and teaching them.

Most often, young female wolves looked after the pups. This was true of Zando's family and it was here that a strong relationship began between Wakan and Acayla.

In the early summer the pups matured and ventured farther away from the den.

Now that they were able to travel short distances, the adult wolves began teaching them how to hunt small game such as squirrels, rabbits and birds.

When they no longer needed the protection of the den, it was time to move the young family to the rendezvous site.

Zando scouted out an ideal location. It was a clearing a few miles away, surrounded by trees near a small creek which flowed into the river.

The spot was hidden from view of passing hunters and would offer protection for the pups until they were able to run and hide if pursued by man.

Life for the pups changed dramatically.

They no longer had the protective home they knew in the den.

The family found shelter in the trees and along ravines, often hiding under overhanging rocks or in small caves during rainstorms.

But Wakan, Sapa, Ohake and Nehma were not concerned about shelter. They were at an age when the world was new and exciting.

Playing games was the most important thing in their lives and they found willing yearlings and adults to help them enjoy chasing, wrestling, and rolling in the grass.

They soon learned that when they wanted someone to play with them they either jumped on an unsuspecting adult who was trying to rest, or approach their intended playmate by bowing down low with their front legs flat on the ground.

If that didn't work, they repeated the procedure or leaped about in a zigzag fashion until they attracted the attention of the older wolves.

Wakan and the others found that yearlings were especially willing to play since it gave them a chance at a second childhood.

The youngsters also learned the sound which attracted playmates. At their age, sounds became very important as they developed their voices and vocabulary.

Wakan played rougher than the other three. Sometimes he played with his litter-mates, but he preferred the company of yearlings and adults.

Often he chose to aggressively attack the older wolves. Just as often he was reprimanded and overpowered by the grown-ups. He did not give up, however, and learned to take advantage whenever the opportunity presented itself.

He tried to participate in every activity of the older wolves, including scent marking and howling.

When the other pups were not interested in playing or when older wolves were not watching, he spent his time investigating the area until he found something to play with.

He picked up sticks and carried them around in his mouth, poking the others until someone chased him in an attempt to take it away.

This usually started a whole new round of romping and rough-housing.

The purpose of the game was to keep control of the stick.

Often the youngster threw the stick or a piece of hide into the air and tried to catch it, or be the first to retrieve it when it fell.

They spent nearly all their waking hours expending their boundless energy running, chasing, pouncing, fighting, and chewing on everything.

This developed their bodies as well as their skills.

The adults took turns playing with the youngsters, and even though they had a great deal of patience with them, they often grew weary of the pups limitless energy.

Wakan tested the good nature of his elders, who, when they grew weary of his constant challenges, growled and barred their teeth at him.

Wolves seldom use force to discipline their young. Simple messages are transmitted which make violence unnecessary.

To an observer, the snarls and showing of teeth by an adult seems harsh. To wolf pups, this is a clear communication that they have gone far enough and should find someone else to bother or go away.

Wolf play establishes closeness within the pack. It is an integral part of their lessons. From this the family is bonded and a relationship of trust and interdependence is established.

Few members of the animal kingdom develop as close an affection and family loyalty as do wolves.

The unity of a wolf pack resembles that of the American Indian which survived and prospered because of close family and tribal ties.

This young family was born into a world where Indians no longer roamed the plains or lived in harmony with nature. Wakan and his brother and sisters knew nothing of the *nature's spirit* that drove the alliance of wolves and Indians. And they had not yet been exposed to the white man and were not aware of the dangers involving them.

The pups had not felt the sting of losing a family member to a hunter's rifle or experienced the pain of watching their kin writhe in death-throes after eating poisoned meat, or stand helplessly by as a fellow wolf struggled to free himself from an inescapable trap.

Unfortunately, these lessons were destined to be a part of their lives in the future.

CHAPTER 5

Summer arrived hot, dry and windy.

The wolf pack spent the better part of their afternoons lying in the shade of trees on the cool sand along the river bank.

Wakan and his litter-mates, now three months old, napped for a time, but became bored and began exploring along the water's edge.

The pups were on one of their endless searches for new adventure, when a mallard drake startled them as he flew low overhead and landed just beyond a patch of cattails.

Curious, Wakan led the tiny pack to the thick growth along the river bank.

Sniffing as they pressed their way through the vegetation, the four came to a small drop-off next to the swiftly moving current.

The pups stuck their black noses through the rushes, eyeing the feathered creatures feeding in the water a few feet away.

The drake and his mate were swimming and periodically diving for food.

The pair's ducklings were stationed near the bank further down the stream, watching their parents' eating ritual.

Sapa's impatience overcame her, "Let's chase them," she growled, and leaped toward the waterfowl.

Instinctively, Wakan followed his sister into the rushing water.

Ohake and Nehma hesitated and watched as Wakan and Sapa made a tremendous splash and started to move downstream with the current.

The ducks escaped, half swimming, half flying to the water's edge where they gathered their young and swam toward the middle of the river away from the danger.

The two pups thrashed around in the water, both submerging as their little legs searched for solid ground.

Before their swimming instincts took over, both were washed downstream several yards, gasping for air as their tiny heads bobbed up and down.

Acayla, alert to the pups' disappearance, heard the disturbance. When the sound of splashing water reached her, she ran through the cattails and leaped into the water.

"Wakan," she cried and quickly grabbed the youngster by the scruff of his neck and swam toward shore.

Laomi, close behind the young female, rescued Sapa the same way.

When they reached the river bank, both pups scrambled out of the water to dry land, shaking and whining.

The excitement lasted only a few seconds.

Ohake and Nehma hid in the tall reeds, afraid to come out.

"Where are the other two?" Laomi inquired.

No one responded.

Laomi began searching and found them crouching safely in the marsh plants.

The commotion woke the remainder of the pack. They ran to investigate.

"Is everyone alright?", Zando inquired as he rushed to the youngsters.

The others arrived and many started licking the pups to help dry them off.

Wolves are comfortable in water. Often they play in creeks or lakes and are not afraid to pursue ducks and geese in water over their heads.

But Wakan and Sapa did not participate in these activities for several weeks following their scary experience.

Instead, they spent the summer exploring their territory on dry land.

The pups were now old enough to follow along with the rest of the family. They were eating solid food and were ready for the nomadic life of a wolf family.

The adults and yearlings took turns watching the pups, seeing to it they were hidden safely when danger approached.

Most of their time was spent learning to stalk and hunt game.

Wakan soon understood that the family did not eat every time they hunted.

"I'm hungry," the growing pup complained.

Zando ignored his sons whining.

"You must understand that we do not capture our prey every time we hunt," the elder wolf explained.

The fact that only about one in ten pursuits resulted in the pack claiming the game they sought, was little comfort to Wakan.

This ratio brought its own lessons to the pups. Since they were weaned, they ate when the rest of the pack ate. If the cached food ran out, their diets depended on their hunting luck.

Often the pack went without eating for a week or more. It was difficult for the pups to adjust but it was an important lesson in their maturing process.

"We must learn to hunt grouse, gophers, prairie dogs and beaver," Zando instructed his offspring.

The youngsters listened intently as their father explained how the family captured the birds and small animals.

"How can we chase a grouse or a duck that flies?" Wakan inquired.

"We must sneak up on them very quietly," Zando answered.

Sometimes the wolves had to compete with coyotes and foxes for these small animals, but this harvest helped them get through the periods when deer and antelope were scarce or difficult to hunt.

The summer was spent moving around the territory in a constant search for food.

There had been very little hunting pressure from the ranchers in the area but the wolf pack kept a watchful eye on their activities. The rolling hills offered the pack opportunities to silently move along a hillside and hide in the tall grass to observe the men working in the hayfields below. Most of the time they did this without the ranchers being aware of their presence.

Wakan and the other youngsters learned that their family spent most days sleeping and spent the nights hunting and exploring.

Night was also the social time for the wolf family. The pups learned to howl and communicate with neighboring families.

If the wind was in the right direction, the wolves could hear other packs several miles away.

During the summer the nights were cool and a lot of playful activity took place. It was an easy life for the four pups.

Wakan spent a great deal of time with his father Zando.

The older wolf patiently instructed Wakan on how to communicate through movements and voice.

Wakan mimicked his father's stance and did his best to raise the pelage hairs on his body like the adult.

He practiced growling and learned that whining provided benefits when the older wolves returned after a kill.

Zando taught Wakan that all members of the pack were important and that they must work together in order to survive.

He instructed him that any stranger was either an enemy or prey.

While hunting, Laomi took over the teaching duties. She included Acayla, the other yearlings, and all four pups in the lessons. She taught them how to distinguish the different scents of game animals and how to follow them.

Laomi was by far the best tracker and hunter. She was almost always the primary hunter for the pack and shared her knowledge with the others.

Before a hunt began, Laomi would walk to a spot of high ground and sniff the air for several minutes.

She then signaled the pack to follow as she led them to a deer crossing on a creek miles away.

She could sense the presence of deer when they were still out of range of the nostrils of the other wolves.

Acayla, still too young to have fully developed her sensitive nose, admired the older female's abilities and worked hard to learn everything she could.

Laomi taught the wolves in the family how to position themselves during the stalk in order to trap the game between the charging wolves.

Surprise was an important element to her success. She continued to instruct the pack to remain out of sight for as long as possible.

Even if the game could catch the scent of the wolves, they could not see the predators and it would gave the pack the extra edge it took for a surprise attack to succeed.

The elusive pronghorn antelope was an excellent example.

This was Wakan's first opportunity to watch a hunt take place.

A couple miles from the hunting site, the smaller pups were left in the care of one of the young females.

"You must stay here while we hunt," Laomi instructed the youngsters.

"Wakan, since you are bigger than the others, you will be allowed to come along," she added.

Wakan's excitement was overflowing. He watched carefully as his mother led the wolf pack to a valley just below a tall butte.

Earlier, another member of the pack spotted a herd of pronghorn grazing on the windward side of the butte and reported this to Zando and Laomi.

Laomi instructed the members of the pack to split into two groups, one to move to the right side of the butte and the other to the left.

"Slowly crawl down the washouts alongside the small clearing where the pronghorn are grazing," Laomi instructed.

Then the female wolf added, "Always keep the wind in front of you."

The wind continued to blow toward the wolves as they approached. The grazing pronghorn had no clue that danger was moving toward them just a few feet away.

Under most circumstances, pronghorn are much too cautious and quick on their feet for wolves. But it had been several days since their last meal of fresh meat and the pack was hungry and willing to take chances.

"Pronghorn always post at least one member of the herd to watch the surrounding territory," Laomi instructed.

She pointed out that these lookouts are conscious of every movement on the prairie. They generally position themselves so they can see extended distances.

The advantage of good vision and alertness are also the pronghorn's downfall. They are extremely curious about everything they see.

On this day, Laomi planned to use this curiosity to lure the pronghorn closer.

Laomi knew the wolves could not outrun the fleet-footed animals. Pronghorn could often outdistance wolves with bursts of speed.

Surprise would be the best way to succeed.

Laomi waited until she knew the hunting wolves had positioned themselves in the ditches on either side of the meadow.

The pronghorn were grazing toward the crest of the buttc, unaware of the potential trap.

Slowly Laomi crawled to the top of the ridge but did not expose herself by peeking over.

Laying flat on the ground, she raised her tail and slowly waved it back and forth so that it was just visible to the pronghorn below.

Instantly the herd's lookout saw the movement.

Several members of the herd, heads erect and ears pointing toward the waving motion on the hilltop, moved closer to get a better view.

They were now walking along the narrowest part of the grassy land strip between the washed out ditches where the wolves were waiting.

Sensing the exact location of the pronghorn without looking, every member of the wolf pack exploded out of the ditches into the center of the herd.

The attack was a complete surprise.

Their curiosity distracted them just long enough for the wolves to gain the extra seconds needed to be successful.

Frightened, the pronghorn turned and sped away. Leaping high to avoid the attack, the animals scattered in every direction.

The lead animal was the closest and became the chosen target for the wolves. This was their only chance.

Skola, the strong beta male, was the first to reach the antelope. He lunged for the rear leg, cutting the hamstring with one quick slash of his powerful jaws.

Acayla slammed into the other side of the animal, knocking him off balance just long enough for Katoh, another female, to clasp her jaws around the pronghorn's neck.

With three wolves attacking simultaneously, the surprised animal panicked and lost its balance.

This was the break the attacking wolves needed.

With three fierce wolves firmly attached to its body, the pronghorn could not get up from the ground.

Struggling, the animal lashed out with its front hooves, striking a fourth female, Zizi, on the shoulder.

The sharp hoof cut the young female's skin and bruised her muscle. Even though she was injured, Zizi quickly got up and helped hold the thrashing animal to the ground while Katoh finished tearing the antelope's jugular.

Other members of the pack arrived moments later to help rip open the pronghorn's belly.

While Zando and Laomi did not participate in the kill, they arrived in time to exercise their right to eat the first fresh meat from the animal.

Wakan, excited over all the activity, had witnessed his first successful hunt.

Prior to this time all four pups had to remain far away from the hunting activity.

Now, the young pup watched intently, anxious to bite into the flesh of the dead animal.

In his excitement, Wakan approached the pronghorn's carcass only to be driven away by his snarling father and mother who were busy eating.

Wakan was frightened and ran away with his ears pinned back and his tail tucked between his hind legs.

This was another lesson he learned about the rank of wolves in the pack. He would have to wait his turn to eat until last since he was the youngest member present. This rule, he found, was strictly enforced.

CHAPTER 6

It was October.

Indian Summer.

The days were warm and the nights were cool.

The wolf pups were maturing, now five months old.

The hunting and stalking lessons continued. Most of the time it was fun because there was a lot of frolicking and rolling around in the grass.

With colder weather approaching, the wolf pack became serious about teaching the youngsters about hunting for survival.

It was vital for each of them to learn the skills of detecting, tracking and capturing game, even though they would not be on their own for at least two more years.

Wakan's comprehension was keener than the other pups and he never seemed to tire of the learning experiences.

Sapa followed as long as she could, but tired more easily than her bigger brother.

Ohake and Nehma, still quite immature, spent most of their time playing or resting.

Each pup discovered they could communicate with one another and with other wolves.

They learned to communicate by the position of their body, by wrinkling their brow and by showing their teeth in certain ways, as well as by voice.

Some of the signals came naturally. Others had to be learned through discipline.

When they began to develop their winter coat of adult hair, still another method of communicating was taught.

The pups watched carefully as adults sent messages to one another simply by raising certain hairs on their bodies.

Every member of the pack participated in the communication lessons.

Wakan watched as the yearling pups ran up to one another and lowered the front part of their bodies, put their rear end and tails high in the air, and smiled.

The wolves they approached would begin to run around in circles, chasing their tails or the tails of a nearby wolf, and the games would begin.

The pups learned there were several forms of smiling. A broad grin communicated friendliness and showed that the smiling wolf did not want to fight or challenge anyone.

The pups learned to make their ears stand erect when listening or asking another wolf to play.

The most unruly part of a pups body however is the tail. Most pups wag their tails constantly and are prime targets for play.

Wakan and Sapa would start the process by biting each other's tail while running around in circles.   The other pups, anxious to join in the fun, would jump on the two, forcing them to let go. Soon all four were in a line, each holding on to the tail of the wolf in front.

Greeting was another important part of communicating.

When members of the pack were gone for a period of time, the remaining wolves would welcome them joyously upon their return.

Zando was used to receiving such a greeting since all members of the pack deferred to him as the alpha male.

This greeting involved nipping around the mouth and face of the returning animal and by lying down on their backs beneath the leader's feet.

The pups learned that this was a sure way to get the returning wolf to regurgitate food for them. Wolves used this method to carry large quantities of food for those members who could not go on the hunting expeditions.

Members of Zando's family always provided food for those too old or too young to accompany them.

Wakan entertained the older members of the pack with his attempts to emulate his father.

Alpha males and females always mark the pack's territory by lifting their legs and urinating on objects along the territorial lines.

This practice is as old as the species. It is used to mark the territory, notifying intruders that this area is occupied and visitors are not welcome.

Zando marked several areas along the trail separating their territory from others. Then Wakan stood unsteadily on three legs while he urinated. Concentrating on wetting the small stump, the youngster lost his balance and fell on his side.

Other wolves rushed up to him, nuzzling him and observing that he not only fell over but missed the stump entirely.

Wakan was determined and continued to practice.

Zando was in the process of teaching Wakan these lessons one afternoon when he spotted a strange wolf approaching.

Wakan was curious since he had never seen one who was not a member of their family.

He watched intently as his father challenged the approaching wolf.

The large gray stranger seemed anxious to come close. Zando however quickly ran to cut off the oncoming intruder before he could reach the inner circle of the pack.

Wakan noticed his father walk stiff-legged for a short distance.

Holding his tail high in the air, Zando raised the fur on his back, and showed his long ivory-colored fangs.

Wakan was impressed.

He had seen this done only in play or during mock challenges within the pack. But this was not play.

It frightened the other pups, but Wakan was too inquisitive to be afraid.

Zando's gray eyes flashed as he looked directly at the approaching wolf. His hostility penetrated the atmosphere between the two animals.

"Do not come any closer," Zando warned.

The on-coming wolf challenged Zando by staring directly back at him.

This was new to Wakan. No member of the pack ever looked directly at Zando's eyes for more than a moment.

The challenge angered Zando. Snarling and teeth bared, he charged the gray wolf, biting him on the neck and pushing him over with his heavy body.

The two engaged in a brief, but intense, exchange of bites and shoves with their forepaws.

Skola quickly rushed to help Zando. The other members of the family also joined the attack.

Within minutes, a fierce battle broke out. The intruder was overwhelmed but fought back strongly.

Finally, realizing he would not be able to overcome the odds, the gray wolf broke loose from the group and started running.

Several members of the pack, led by Skola, pursued him, biting his hind legs and sides as he made his escape.

After running several yards, Zando's wolves stopped the chase and allowed the intruder to go free.

Although injured by the severe bites, the gray wolf continued running at high speed until he disappeared over a nearby hill.

Wakan realized that this wolf had ignored the early warning signals in the form of the pack leaders' scent markings.

He also realized that the wolf paid for his ignorance and might have been killed had Zando not signaled the wolves to allow him to go free.

By the time the territorial fight ended, the sun was setting.

Zando trotted on to a small hill nearby and raised his head into the air and howled a strong boisterous song.

Within moments the entire pack joined the alpha wolf on the hill, each adding his voice to the chorus.

Wakan tried to imitate the sound but failed miserably.

For some reason he just could not get the sound right. Often when the other wolves were howling, he tried, but failed to complete the melodious notes.

He wanted to learn to howl more than anything else.

Learning to howl properly was important because howling held so many meanings.

This vocal exhibition denoted victory and added emphasis to the territorial claim of the pack.

Wakan wanted to be a part of that victory.

Howling was also used to call family members together when game was spotted.

It was done to announce a successful hunting expedition.

Howling let other packs know when a territory was occupied, and it was part of socializing, allowing individual wolves the opportunity to let their voices be heard.

Wakan watched and listened as the adults and yearlings held their heads high with dignity.

He practiced endlessly, much to the dismay of the others in the pack.

Wakan stretched his neck, formed his mouth and pushed the noise from deep within his chest.

What came out was often a high pitched squeal or a growl.

After listening to him practice for several minutes, his mother or one of the other adults would grow weary of the constant noise and push him to get him to stop.

Since adult discipline was usually gentle, it sometimes took several attempts to get Wakan to quiet down.

The youngster was especially fascinated when another wolf would howl in the distance. He immediately stood up and tried to return the signal.

Time would improve his voice, but he was impatient for that.

Not all Wakan's lessons came easily.

He had trouble accepting the superiority of any wolf other than his father and mother.

The older members ranked much higher in authority than this young pup.

Even though he surpassed his litter-mates in every way, and accomplished much of what the yearlings could do, he was still considered a pup by the older wolves.

In his enthusiasm, Wakan would keep his tail raised when he approached his elders. Because of his rank in the pack, he was supposed to keep his tail lowered, his head down, and his ears laid close to his head.

Most of the adults accepted Wakan's playful enthusiasm and overlooked this trait. Others, however, resented this mannerism and became impatient with him.

They snarled and bit him lightly and pushed him down, forcing the youngster to roll over in submission.

Zando and Laomi did not interfere. Often they also dispensed discipline in order to bring the aggressive pup into line.

But Wakan's spirit was strong and he accepted the reprimand without a whimper.

CHAPTER 7

Crisp days of autumn came to the prairie.

The cottonwood and oak leaves turned bright gold and "rattled" with each gust of wind.

During the first months of their lives, Wakan, Sapa, Ohake, and Nehma knew no threats other than an occasional visiting wolf. They had been sheltered from the dangers of the outside world.

In the pre-dawn hours of one cold morning, several members of the pack raced into the rendezvous area. In their excitement, the wolves were noisily yapping and barking.

Wakan, just awakening, could not understand what was happening.

Zizi, a yellow female approached Zando, the guard hairs on her body were raised.

Through a series of growls and whines, Zizi communicated, "Mayach has been caught in a trap!"

Zando immediately determined that the traps were located near a deer trail which the wolves normally followed.

Zizi indicated the wolf was still alive.

Zando signaled, "I must go at once."

It was the duty of the alpha wolf to investigate the danger.

He ordered Skola to stand guard over the remainder of the pack until his return.

As Zando left the rendezvous area, Wakan followed. In the excitement, no one noticed as the youngster quietly slipped out behind his father.

Zando was determined to check on the plight of the young member of his pack and was too preoccupied to notice Wakan trailing along behind.

In the darkness, Wakan had difficulty seeing his father on the trail ahead. His sense of smell was not yet fully developed and he soon lost his father's scent.

Zando moved swiftly across the prairie toward the wooded area near a large creek where the wolf pack often hunted. Unaware his son was following, he disappeared into the darkness of the early morning.

Wakan was lost.

He followed what he thought was his father's trail and soon became disoriented.

In the blackness, he became confused and could not remember how to return home.

His first reaction was to howl. Realizing that a member of the pack had fallen into the hands of the hunters, he decided to remain silent.

He traveled at least two miles before be decided to stop and wait until sunrise.

Even though he was only seven months old, the young wolf knew he should not panic and draw attention to himself.

Wakan found a sheltered area near some trees and settled down to wait until light came. He would then be able to find his way back to his family.

Meanwhile Zando advanced toward the trapped wolf with caution.

He knew the wolf hunters would be checking their traps early in the morning since wolves usually were caught during nighttime hours.

Zando realized that if the white men saw him near the traps he might be shot, and he knew he could accidently step in nearby traps.

Moving slowly, he smelled every strange scent, stopping periodically to check the wind.

It was beginning to get light.

Zando realized he would be in danger if he continued to follow the deer trail where the pack member had been trapped.

He moved silently through the trees, a few feet off the trail.

He heard voices about a hundred yards ahead. The men were talking as they rode along the trail. He followed their sounds, keeping well hidden.

Suddenly they stopped talking.

Then a man's shout pierced the quiet morning air as a rifle shot rang out.

Then another.

The two men began talking loudly, as they ran down the deer trail toward the trapped wolf.

Zando moved to within fifty yards of the fracas. The sun was now peaking over the horizon, lighting the area where the hunters had set the traps.

He could see one of the men holding up Mayach's body by the tail.

Zando's instinct was to help his fellow wolf. But it was too late.

The rancher's horses snorted loudly and looked in Zando's direction.

Busy with their newly claimed prize, the riders ignored the horse's warnings that another wolf was in the area.

This gave Zando an opportunity to move away unnoticed.

Saddened by the loss of Mayach, Zando was nevertheless alert to the dangers posed by the hunters. He quickly moved back across the prairie to the rendezvous area.

His thoughts were still on Mayach when he rejoined the rest of the pack.

Frantically, Laomi met him at the edge of the area.

"Is Wakan with you?" she questioned.

"No," he communicated.

The other members of the pack gathered near.

Zando took a moment to communicate that Mayach had been killed.

Laomi and Acayla, expecting this report after Zizi imparted the information to them, centered their concern on Wakan.

"Did he follow you?" Laomi inquired.

"I do not know," Zando related.

In order to calm the two female wolves, Zando conveyed, "He must be somewhere near here since I did not see him following me or hear any shots other than those which destroyed Mayach."

Worried, Laomi replied, "What about traps?"

Zando did not answer.

"We must all search for Wakan!" Laomi exclaimed.

Most of the wolf pack milled around the clearing uncertain about what to do.

To eliminate the confusion, Zando stood in the sunlight and communicated his message to the entire group.

"We have already lost one member of the family," he admonished. "We must be careful of the hunters who are out there looking for wolves this morning."

Zando continued, "Wakan is missing and we must find him."

The alpha male gathered those wolves who were nearby as he made his hasty departure.

"Did anyone see Wakan?" he inquired.

None of the wolves responded.

Zando then led Laomi, Skola and a small group of others to the trail he followed when he left the rendezvous area.

Zizi and Katoh were assigned the job of watching over the other three pups.

As they moved toward the trail, Laomi noticed that Acayla was not with them.

Believing she was concerned about the safety of the other pups, Laomi gave no further thought to her whereabouts.

Acayla had left the rendezvous area immediately after Zando revealed Wakan was not with him.

She studied every scent, searching for the young pup. She was near panic, but held her composure as she strained her eyes, ears and nostrils for any hint of Wakan.

"The dew is erasing strong scents," she lamented.

"But I will find him," she reassured herself.

Acayla was at least a mile ahead of the other wolves when she picked up a familiar aroma.

Excitement gripped her. She wanted to let the others know she was on Wakan's trail.

Afraid to howl or make loud noises which would attract hunters, she moved silently through the tall grass searching for her precious friend.

Approaching a small grove of trees, Acayla sniffed the air convinced that Wakan was nearby.

Passing the end of a gigantic cottonwood tree trunk, Acayla felt a heavy blow strike her back.

She tumbled sideways into the grass.

Quickly she jumped up and turned, ready to attack who ever had pushed her over.

Wakan suddenly leaped through the air, landing in Acayla's face.

Both wolves tumbled into a pile of newly fallen leaves.

Still surprised and angry, Acayla immediately regained her feet and jumped on Wakan, biting him hard on the back of his neck.

Shocked by her fierce response, Wakan did not know how to react.

He immediately rolled over on his back, submitting to her authority.

Acayla was angry at Wakan for playing games and scaring her.

The young wolf was unaware of her concern over his whereabouts and her fear for his life.

Wakan jumped to his feet when Acayla did not pursue her attack, licking her face and expressing his joy over their reunion.

Acayla was relieved. Wakan was safe and healthy.

The two wolves turned toward the rendezvous area on a course which would take them directly in the path of the other family members.

In a few minutes, Acayla spotted Zando and Laomi.

Leaping high in the air through the tall grass, Acayla informed the alpha pair that she had found their lost son.

The reunion was joyful. Tails wagging and ears piqued, everyone gathered around Wakan, welcoming him to the safety of the family.

The wolves played and scampered around, momentarily forgetting that a member of the pack was trapped and shot by hunters earlier in the day.

CHAPTER 8

Zando spent hours with Wakan, teaching him how to use his instincts and learn strategies to carry out the work of *nature's spirit*.

This is how Wakan began to recognize the spiritual relationship between wolves and other wild animals.

The relationship manifests itself during the hunt. In the final moments before the kill, the hunter and the hunted reveal their historic roles in the balance of nature.

Wakan learned that it is the wolf's function to be the custodian of the animal herds and to help keep them strong and healthy. For the most part, wolves killed diseased, maimed or lame members in the wildlife herd. Those who fell into this category knew their fate.

While there was often a chase and resistance, in the final moments, the prey submitted to the predator.

Zando's pack had done an excellent job of cleaning up the countryside. Very few lame or diseased animals remained.

But hunger was a constant companion of wolves and the pack was constantly alert to opportunities to bring down prey.

One such occasion took place just before the heavy snows of winter began. Some of the wolf scouts picked up the scent of elk. The animals were moving through the aspen and pine trees which covered the long valley at the foot of the buttes in the center of the pack's territory.

Elk seldom ventured this far from the mountains but the small herd migrated away from their normal range in the high country. The herd consisted of a magnificent old bull, two yearling bulls and a half dozen cows.

More than likely the older bull had been driven out of an area by a stronger male. Apparently he managed to gather a few stray females and their yearlings as he moved out of his former range.

The wolf pack anxiously awaited the opportunity to hunt these splendid creatures.

Wakan and the other pups were now old enough to accompany the adults on the hunting adventure.

There was a sense of excitement as Laomi laid out the plan to attack the elk.

Through low growls and gestures, the alpha female instructed Skola and Caska to circle behind the herd on the left side of the valley.

She directed Kahnge and Oshota to circle around to the right. Their job was to form a wedge at the wide area of the valley and slowly drive the elk herd down. The wolves instinctively knew the elk would stay in the deepest cover for protection. They counted on this to help them accomplish their goal of keeping the herd from splitting up.

Once these four had been deployed, Laomi assigned Zizi, Ocha-meae, Zando and Acayla to be the attack wolves. She strategically placed them at the narrow portion of the valley where the elk would emerge. This group was led by Zando.

These wolves were placed just below a rock drop-off. Laomi knew the elk would hesitate before picking their way through the rocks. That would be the time to strike.

Laomi, Wakan, and the other pups stationed themselves a few yards farther down the narrow passage below the rock drop-off.

When the elk slowed to jump over the rocks, Laomi planned to step into the open in front of them. This would momentarily surprise the animals. This was when the others would attack from the side.

The wolves following the herd would not be close enough to be in on the initial attack. But they would be in position to chase any elk which turned back. This was the part of the strategy that provided an opportunity to bring down another animal in the event the initial attack failed.

Laomi's plans usually provided more than one chance for success. She taught each wolf in the hunting party to be constantly alerted to opportunities in each hunt.

Skola led the group pursuing the elk through the trees. He was a strong, intelligent five year old wolf who had many battle scars because of his aggressive nature.

Known as one of the bravest hunters in the pack, he kept the others in his platoon in line. He took charge of positioning the members of the drive pack near the head of the valley, just where the trees became dense.

The pushers moved noisily through the woods, trying to alert the elk to their presence, but not frightening them into panic.

They could hear the elk start to move. The wind was at the back of Skola and his companions. Their scent drifted toward the elk.

Since the wolves did not display any real aggression, the elk leisurely made their way through the srub oak and pine toward an exit they knew was just ahead.

Laomi selected the attack location correctly. With the wind blowing from behind the elk, the wolves could hear the snapping branches and the clattering hooves. The attack team also picked up the scent and the sounds of the herd.

Since breeding season was over, the bull had allowed the two younger bulls to tag along with his harem. On this occasion, one of the young bulls was sent ahead to lead the herd down the valley away from the danger.

The old bull's instinct always kept him alert for other dangers so he had the larger of the two young bulls move through the woods just ahead of him as a decoy. The sly old bull moved down the valley behind his entourage, keeping an eye on the pesky wolves in the woods behind him.

Near the bottom of the valley, the rock piles became larger and the small elk herd picked its way carefully.

Just as the young bull and a fat cow reached a small drop-off in the floor of the valley, the young bull suddenly snorted and turned back. He spotted Laomi and Wakan standing on the trail twenty yards ahead.

He whirled around bumping into the cow following close behind. Both momentarily lost their balance. This was the opportunity the attack wolves had been waiting for.

They instinctively selected the cow, knowing that even a young bull's antlers could strike a fatal blow.

Acayla lunged for the rear flank of the cow. Zando tore the tendons in back of the powerful hind leg. Ocha-meae lunged at the cows neck, inflicting deep slashes before the animal could regain her balance.

Zizi attacked the animal's head, biting firmly on the elk's nostrils. Fighting to free herself, the huge cow threw her head into the air. Zizi steadfastly clamping her jaws, closing off the cow's breathing passages.

Laomi and Wakan arrived seconds later, biting and tearing at any exposed part of the cow. The massive animal lost her footing among the rocks in a desperate attempt to flee from the aggressors.

It was no use.

The attack came too swiftly.

Attempting to fend off the wolves at her hind legs, she left her head exposed. Laomi leaped to the cow's throat, her powerful jaws tearing a gaping hole in the windpipe and jugular vein.

A moment later the cow, which outweighed her attackers tenfold, lay on her side, her life draining away.

The kill took less than ten minutes.

The chase wolves arrived just as the battle was finished. They could see the attack was successful, so they allowed the remainder of the elk to escape.

Wakan's participation in the elk attack was that of an observer standing close to his mother's side. He wanted to be in on the kill, but he was disciplined by Laomi and forced to stay out of the fight.

The young wolf remained alert during the entire episode. He watched and learned the tactics of capturing a large animal by using the landscape to their advantage.

Each of the wolves took turns eating according to their rank.

Laomi and Zando moved in to claim the prize first, tearing the heavy, leathery hide from the elk, exposing the flesh and intestines. The liver was divided between the two of them, their reward for being alpha male and female of the pack. The wolf pack feasted on the elk carcass.

After Zando and Laomi finished eating, the older members ate their fill. The rank among the yearlings and two-year-olds was still being decided and these wolves snapped at each other in order to get the best pieces of meat.

Wakan decided it was time he asserted his rank, but he was pushed away by the older wolves who had more experience in defending the kill.

The family ate for several hours, then finally filled with the sweet flesh of the elk, many rested in the nearby trees.

Others took chunks of meat to a safe storage area. The weather was turning colder and it was necessary to save some of the meat for leaner times.

After several hours, having had their fill, the wolves returned to the rendezvous site with their stomachs distended.

CHAPTER 9

As the winter months passed, cold weather continued between each snowstorm.

Huge snowdrifts filled the valleys and piled high in the few groves of trees that existed in the area.

Often, deer herds were trapped in the trees where they took refuge from the storms.

The cold weather and constant winds put a thick crust on the snow making it possible for the wolves to walk over the drifts in search of the wildlife.

Food was scarce, and the threat of the hunters was constantly present. This often kept the wolf pack on the run and unable to hunt efficiently.

"Everyone must be alert at all times," Zando declared.

He gave his warning to the remaining members of the pack now numbering eleven adults and four pups.

The loss of Mayach had a severe impact on the group.

He was a skilled hunter and valuable to the success of the family.

"We must communicate with one another regularly," the alpha wolf admonished.

Zando was relating rules to the pack. "To be more efficient, we need to hunt together rather than break up into smaller groups".

Zando realized that the pups were still too young to contribute to the hunting efforts and it would take the combined skills of the entire group of adults to sustain them.

Zando also knew that Skola and Zizi were anxious to break away from the pack and form their own family.

The leader took the two aside and communicated to them that it was important that they continue the close relationship of the entire pack and that they should not leave the pack before the next breeding season.

Skola and Zizi agreed.

"We must remain together one more winter," Zando indicated. "Otherwise we will not be able to bring in enough game to survive."

Zando was anxious to have Wakan mature and replace Skola as the beta male. But that would not happen for another year.

Wakan, the larger of the four weighed about 65 pounds while Ohake, Nehma, and Sapa weighed about 55 pounds.

Part of this rapid development came because Wakan had acquired his adult teeth and could eat larger amounts of meat from the carcasses.

Ohake, Nehma, and Sapa still depended mainly on regurgitated food brought back by the adults.

Now that winter had arrived, the young wolves had to keep up with the older hunters. Wakan accompanied the hunters on their daily searches for food.

The other three often trailed along behind the adults and approached the game animal once it had been killed.

But hunting success continued to elude the wolves.

Single file, the wolves moved throughout the territory, scouting for food.

They seldom went near the ranches but in recent years fences appeared on land which had previously been open range.

Cattle, sheep and horses populated these pastures, interfering with the wolves hunting patterns that had existed for centuries.

The winters deep snow offered an advantage to the wolves. It was much easier for them to follow the deer and antelope. However, it also made the wolves vulnerable to the ranchers since their tracks were also visible to those who constantly pursued them.

As the winter wore on, the pack depended more and more on jack-rabbits and other small game in the area.

While the family was accustomed to a feast and famine existence, this was the longest period without adequate food that most members of the pack had ever experienced.

It was during this period of hunger for Wakan's family that some of them began attacking domestic livestock.

Three members of the pack found a heifer alone along one of the pasture fences.

They circled the animal and attacked it. Within minutes the wolves killed the young cow and had eaten their fill. They returned to the area where the pack was resting with the good news about the kill.

In the early morning hours, just after sunrise, the entire pack ate the first fresh meat they had enjoyed in several weeks.

After the pack gorged themselves, they returned to their hiding area in the thick pine trees three miles away.

The family rested the next two days and did not return to the carcass until two nights later.

Caska led Wakan and Acayla back to the heifer just after sunset.

When they approached the carcass, Caska snarled savagely at the two younger wolves, warning them that he was going to eat first.

Wakan and Acayla lay quietly in the snow, watching Caska eat.

Suddenly, Caska leaped away from the carcass. His mouth was wide open. He made a vain attempt to regurgitate what he had just eaten.

Surprised by Caska's action, Wakan and Acayla stood nearby, afraid to approach the male wolf.

Caska began choking and convulsing. The two younger wolves had never seen anything like it.

The older wolf showed signs of severe pain and began running around in circles, biting the snow in an attempt to wash out his mouth.

He continued the erratic activity for several minutes before stumbling and falling headlong into a small drift.

As Wakan and Acayla approached him, he lay kicking his hind legs, scratching at his stomach.

Afraid to go near the wolf and not understanding what was happening to Caska they both turned back to where the rest of the family was located.

As they approached, the pack was lounging on the south slope of a wooded hillside. Most members had eaten some of the cached meat supply and were full.

Excited, Acayla and Wakan communicated to Zando and Laomi that something terrible had happened to Caska.

Curious, the alpha pair followed Acayla and Wakan back to the wolf lying near the heifer carcass.

Zando warned the others to stay back while he investigated.

Wakan watched his father sniff the now lifeless body of this wolf, cautious and alert to the possibility of a surprise attack from man.

"I have smelled this before," Zando declared. "It is poisoned meat."

A couple of the older adults approached the heifer.

"No one go near the meat," he ordered.

Zando snarled and bit them, forcing them away from the carcass.

Wakan was learning a lesson he would remember for the rest of his life. His older brother, greedy to eat first, approached the dead heifer without first checking for tracks or human scent.

After a few minutes of investigating the area, even Wakan could detect the smell of the humans who had poisoned the critter.

While the wolves wandered around the carcass, Zando made it clear that no one was to ever approach this animal again.

"We must continue to look for wild game," he signaled. "We cannot trust the meat of any animal unless we kill it ourselves."

Then the wolf instructed the pack, "When we kill an animal, we must eat our fill, then store the rest so that men cannot find it and poison it."

It was during this intensive effort by ranchers to rid the range of wolves that another lesson came into focus for the wolf family.

Zando and Laomi had spent considerable time teaching the younger pack members about the danger of traps.

Unfortunately, the lesson did not come soon enough for Wakan and Kahnge.

Wakan was walking a few yards behind Kahnge along a seldom used deer trail covered with a light dusting of snow. Both wolves were well ahead of the other members of the pack, sniffing for scents of deer.

Suddenly, Kahnge stopped near a clump of sage brush. Something did not seem right.

Wakan, alert to Kahnge's curiosity, stood still.

Kahnge carefully circled the sage plant, sniffing the ground but staying clear of the suspected trap setting.

As he circled the trap, keeping a few feet distant, Wakan suddenly heard a loud "snap".

Immediately Kahnge yelped in pain. He had stepped into a steel trap with his left hind leg.

Kahnge's cries alerted the remainder of the pack which came running down the deer path.

Wakan, frightened of what had happened to Kahnge, started to turn away.

Concentrating on his older brother's plight, Wakan was not cautious.

Suddenly his right front foot landed on something unfamiliar. He instantly jerked his foot away from the object, just as the steel jaws of the heavy trap snapped.

His out side toe was caught.

Shrieking with pain, Wakan pulled away from the trap with all his power. He heaved his body back, fearing that he would not escape.

The sharp pain enveloped his entire front leg and he felt burning flashes in his shoulder.

Wakan fell to the ground, unaware that he had freed himself from the trap.

Yake, a two-year-old female, had been following a short distance behind Kahnge and Wakan. She ran in a wide circle around the two wolves while watching them closely.

Not concentrating on where she was running, Yake stepped into a hidden trap with her front leg.

Her loud cries for help blended with Kahnge and Wakan as they filled the air with their shrieks.

Acayla was the first of the pack to reach the area.

Oblivious to everything except Wakan, she rushed to her friend, ignoring the potential danger of other traps.

"You're hurt," she exclaimed.

"My foot, my foot," Wakan cried.

Meanwhile Kahnge continued to snarl and bit at his rear leg in a vain attempt to escape. It was no use.

The trap had snapped tightly over the lower portion of his hip and no matter how hard he struggled, there was no way to get free.

Yake was suffering the same fate. Regarless of how hard she struggled, the trap held fast.

"Do not go near them," Zando ordered.

"Watch out for other traps," Laomi declared, keeping the others back from the unhappy scene.

Acayla lay near Wakan's side as he licked his bleeding paw. Zando and Laomi watched from a distance, fearing for the lives of Acayla and their offspring.

Slowly, Wakan got to his feet and Acayla led him out of the danger area, back along the path to the family who were intently watching the scene before them.

After Wakan reached safety, Zando entered the area, walking in the same path just made by the two younger wolves.

The alpha wolf approached Kahnge who had quit struggling and was lying in distressful pain.

"We are unable to help you," Zando declared sadly.

"I know," Kahnge answered with a whimper.

Zando stood by the side of his older son, licking and nuzzling his face to give him comfort.

Laomi approached Yake with the same news. "We cannot help."

Yake looked at her mother, resigned to her fate.

"We must leave before the hunters come," Zando declared.

He turned and walked carefully around the scents which indicated other traps were set in the area.

After checking on Wakan and seeing that he was okay, Laomi stood for several minutes looking at her children still in caught in the traps. No one bothered her as she bid farewell.

Sadly the pack retraced their steps along the deer path and left their family members to the merciless hunters who would find him later in the day.

As they made their escape, Wakan stopped every few minutes to lick his wounded foot. Acayla also attempted to cleanse the injury, but it was so painful, Wakan snapped at her to keep her away.

The pack continued to travel several miles to an area where they felt safe enough to stop and rest, allowing Wakan to nurse his damaged foot.

When the hunters arrived, Kahnge and Yake were still alive, staring viciously at their captors. The trappers quickly shot them.

As the two men investigated the area, one of them found the trap from which Wakan had escaped.

"Look, we almost caught another one," the trapper commented.

"What did he do, spring the trap?" the other asked.

"No, he got his toe caught," the first hunter answered. "Look at this," he said, holding up the wolf's toe by the claw.

"Too bad we didn't get the whole damn wolf," was the reply.

"Well, with only three toes, at least we'll be able to track him," he concluded.

"That one's marked for life," the other added.

They finished tying Yake and Kahnge with their lariats and dragged the wolves away.

CHAPTER 10

A few weeks after Wakan lost his toe, Ocha-meae, a female member of the pack, died of a gunshot wound.

She was hunting alone about a mile from the rest of the pack when a party of wolfers spotted her and began shooting.

The first few shots missed as the wolf dodged behind rocks and sage brush.

When the shooting stopped, Ocha-meae thought she was safe and began to make her escape by running along the bank of a small creek.

The treeless embankment offered her no protection and she was exposed to the riflemen who were sitting on the ridge on the opposite side of the stream.

One of the riders fired a shot. Ocha-meae was knocked from her feet.

Pain paralyzed her rear legs. The adrenalin began pumping and she was able to pull her body into a washout with her strong front legs.

Her wound was in the rear flank. The bullet cut through her hip and into her lower intestines. The pain was unbearable.

Ocha-meae crawled several yards before the hunters were able to ride down from the ridge and cross the creek to get to her.

The men lost track of the exact spot where she had been wounded and searched for nearly an hour without finding a trace.

After sunset, Ocha-meae crawled back toward the area where the pack had been resting that afternoon.

Stopping every few minutes to lick her wounds, the one mile trip took several hours.

Acayla was the first to spot the wounded female. She heard the shots earlier in the afternoon and had begun to look for her friend.

Acayla ran to the female's side and started to lick her wound. The cries of pain sounded an alarm to the other family members who also came running to assist.

Wakan followed Acayla but stopped suddenly when he heard Ocha-meae's loud whines. This was his first experience witnessing the pain suffered from a gunshot wound.

Everyone in the pack gathered around the wounded female. Their reactions ranged from whining in sympathy to barking and howling in frustration. The anguish and pain they were seeing were overwhelming.

All through the night the members of the pack tried to make Ocha-meae comfortable, but within a few hours the wounded wolf died.

Wakan could feel his anger toward man intensifying. He recalled Caska's painful death by poison, then Kange and Yake's futile cries for help, and his own trap-inflicted injury. All this increased his feeling of loathing, since he realized man killed without purpose and he did not understand *Nature's Spirit*.

Now Ocha-meae's death simply added to his pain.

The silence was broken when Zando, and other family members began howling in the darkness, lamenting the loss and notifying other wolves of the danger which continued to exist in the territory.

The hunters and trappers persisted throughout the winter, keeping the pack moving constantly.

When breeding season arrived, the professional wolfers brought dogs into the area to track the wolves. The pack split up into smaller groups and moved continuously in order to keep the dogs confused.

This interrupted Laomi's and the other female's normal estrus cycle. Zando and Laomi did not breed.

Separated, the wolves pattern of life changed dramatically. Zando and Laomi kept the pups and Acayla in one group. Skola and Zizi led the remainder of the pack to another part of the territory a few miles away.

Periodically the group met to hunt and feast on their success. Nearly all the hunting was done at night. During the day Zando, Laomi, Acayla and the pups spent their time hiding in the hundreds of small caverns in the Cave Hills.

Skola stayed in the heavy timber along a creek.

The family communicated every night by howling, letting the other group know where they were and what was happening.

Zando's plan was to keep the pack hidden for a few weeks to make the ranchers and wolfers believe the pack had moved on.

The plan worked. The wolves managed to stay out of sight and away from the pastures where hunters were usually seen. After two months of not seeing a trace of wolves, the daily hunts ceased and only the traps and poison laced carcasses were left.

Zando and Laomi continued to warn all members of the pack not to approach the poisoned meat.

"Traps will have fresh meat nearby," the alpha male warned, hoping the younger wolves would heed the admonition as they left their hiding places each day in search of food.

Wakan and the other pups endured many days without food. The resourceful young wolf did manage to capture a few squirrels who had made the mistake of running between trees on warm days.

As spring approached there were more grouse in the area and the wolves dined on the feathered prey and caught rabbits whenever they could.

Wakan continued to have trouble with his right paw. The harsh winter did not allow the foot to heal immediately and he developed a slight limp because it was sensitive to the cold and constant use.

Zando gathered his family together and brought them back down on the prairie to their old familiar territory.

It was a happy reunion for the wolves. The clan gathered together, anxious to get on with their normal lives. In the days that followed, several successful hunts were achieved and the pack looked forward to a secure summer.

On a mild day in May, the pack was moving close to the calving pasture belonging to one of the large ranches. They were crossing the area to reach a resting place in a grove of trees a few miles away.

Loping at a steady pace, the pack was strung out for over a hundred yards.

Zando was in the lead, followed by Laomi, then Acayla and Skola, the four pups and the remainder of the pack.

Skirting the crest of a hill, Zando kept a good deal of distance between themselves and the grazing cattle.

Suddenly, two men on horseback rode over the top of the small hill that the pack was skirting.

Zando immediately warned the others as he bolted away from the intruders to lead them in the opposite direction.

The riders followed.

Keeping an eye on the horsemen, who were still too far away to shoot, Zando urged the pack to spread out and remain at a safe distance from the danger.

Moments later, two more riders appeared on the ridge in front of the escaping wolves.

Zando whirled around and warned his family of the new danger.

One avenue of escape remained, but they had to retrace the path they had traveled just a few minutes before.

As Zando and Laomi urged the pack to safety, a third pair of riders cut off their retreat.

Zando tried to keep the family from getting too close to the riders who were closing in.

The alpha male spotted an escape route where several wolves could remove themselves from the danger.

Their only chance was to split up.

Zando called Skola to his side and instructed him to lead Acayla and two of the pups down to a washout which was hidden from the view of the riders.

He urged Laomi to take another route with Wakan and Sapa.

At the same time, the alpha male led Zizi, Katoh and Oshota toward an opening between the first and second set of riders hoping they would pursue them and not search for the other family members he had sent to safety.

The riders closed in on Zando and the three wolves following him.

Shots echoed off the surrounding hills as the hunters fired at the small pack circling in the sights of their guns.

There was no escape.

Each rifleman picked a target and fired, first wounding the wolves, then finally killing all four.

Skola and his small group ran up the washout to the hill opposite where the shooting had taken place.

Laomi, Wakan and Sapa managed to stay close to the ground and remained out of sight in a washout.

Laomi led her son and daughter in the opposite direction along a small ridge, keeping them out of sight of the riders.

Once they reached the safety of the hills above the valley, Laomi turned to see what had happened to her mate. She saw the hunters gathering around the bodies of Zando, Oshota, Katoh, and Zizi lying in the grass.

"Zando is dead," she cried as she heard the final cracks of the high powered rifles.

Then there was silence.

Laomi brought Wakan and Sapa to her side as she stood at the crest of the hill.

The hunters were kicking her mate and the three others. They were already celebrating, holding Zando up by his tail.

One hunter, uncertain of whether his bullets had fatally injured Zizi, raised his rifle at close range and fired into her skull. Wakan could see his mother flinch at the sound.

Katoh and Oshota were being tied to the saddle horns with lariats. The hunters were getting ready to drag the family members away to collect the bounty.

Wakan and his mother stood in full view of the men below, not caring about their safety. They watched as a man tied a rope to Zando and began dragging him behind his horse.

Laomi ached for Zando and anger rose up in her heart for the cruel way they treated her mate.

Wakan became so angry at the scene below that he started to run toward the hunters, growling fiercely.

Laomi ran to his side and knocked him off balance on the grassy hillside.

"Stay here, we cannot help him," she admonished her son.

Determined, Wakan got to his feet and started down the hill again, too young to realize he could not take revenge on armed men.

Again, Laomi knocked her pup off his feet, this time standing over him, pinning him to the ground.

"Stay," she ordered.

Wakan remained silent and indicated he would not get up and run down the hill again. When Laomi stepped off him, he moved slowly back to the top of the hill.

Sapa, shocked by what had happened, stood staring at the scene below.

The trio spent several minutes watching the hunters drag their family members in the direction of their ranch.

Then Wakan motioned, "Where are Acayla and the others?"

They began to survey the countryside looking for any of the other family members. They saw no one.

For several minutes the three stood at the top of the hill. Then realizing they might be spotted by other hunters, Wakan nudged Laomi and Sapa to lay down.

Laomi lay apart from the others, quietly watching for a sign that the rest of her family was okay.

Silently waiting for Zando to appear on the horizon, she hoped for a miracle.

It was not to be.

Finally, Wakan urged his mother and sister to follow him as he moved off the hillside.

Zando had taught Wakan well. The time the two spent together had prepared the younger wolf for future responsibilities, but not for these circumstances.

Now, just a little over a year old, Wakan was hardly ready to assume leadership. But he knew he must accept what fate had dealt him. He would have to take care of his mother and sister and get them to safety.

He scanned the horizon for Acayla and the others but he did not have time to search for them.

As he was contemplating where they should go, Sapa indicated that riders were heading toward them.

Wakan knew it was time to leave this territory and find a safe place somewhere else.

He didn't know where he was going, he simply wanted to get his mother and sister away from the danger.

Each time the wolves reached the top of a hill and looked back, they saw that the riders continued their pursuit. There was no time to plan a strategy, Wakan knew he must lead what was left of his family to safety.

Wakan headed north, away from the scene where they witnessed the end of Zando's life.

As they ran away from their territory, Wakan thought of Acayla and what had happened to her. He realized his life would never be the same again. Man had dealt a fatal blow, one he would never forget.

Acayla, meanwhile, was following Skola's leadership. Their little group included Nehma and Ohake.

Riders were also pursuing them, forcing them to head south. For several hours the hunters continued to follow them. Each time Skola tried to stop or turn back, the riders gained ground on them and would begin shooting.

Finally, recognizing that they could not go back to find the rest of the family, the beta male led his dependents to a new area, never before explored by his pack.

CHAPTER 11

Wakan, Laomi, and Sapa successfully escaped the pursuing hunters by maintaining a constant loping gait throughout the rest of the day and far into the night.

Finally, after twelve hours of constant travel, the three stopped along a small creek to drink and rest.

Wakan's paw ached from the continuous running. He was beginning to limp and needed to rest his foot before going any further. His leg muscles burned with every step, but he did not tell the others.

He could see that Laomi was deeply troubled over Zando's death and the disappearance of Acayla and the two pups. He did not want to add to her grief by complaining.

Wakan comforted his mother and sister as the three wolves lay close together, hidden from view in a grove of choke-cherry bushes.

As he rested, Wakan's thoughts turned to Acayla. He refused to believe that she had been killed.

In Wakan's mind he held an image of her. He could visualize her beautiful light gray coat glistening in the sunlight.

There were darker gray hairs on her shoulders and hips and patches of black fur around her ears. Her muzzle was white and slightly shorter than most wolves. Her black nose and piercing yellow eyes accented her beautiful face.

The young female always stood erect, head held high. She was constantly alert.   The light gray pelt was accentuated by the nearly pure white legs and feet.

Wakan missed Acayla and hoped that she was safe. But for now, the young male had to assume the responsibility of leadership.

In the panic of escaping the hunters, the group did not have a destination in mind when they left the pasture where the massacre took place. Their sole intention was to put distance between themselves and the danger.

As they moved northward into new territory, Wakan found himself making the decisions for his mother and sister.

Laomi, distraught over the sudden death of Zando, simply followed along and was not responsive when Wakan sought her input into which direction to take or whether to rest or continue on.

Sapa, overwhelmed by the events of the past few days, also looked to Wakan for guidance.

The route Wakan chose transported the group across a desolate, unpopulated area, away from all signs of humans.

Three days after the murder of their family, the trio arrived in the North Dakota Badlands.

As they entered the eerie landscape, dawn was breaking over the horizon.

"We're safe now," Wakan indicated to Laomi and Sapa.

He led them to a small washed out indentation on the side of a huge eroded hill. Wakan's first concern was to find a safe haven and rest.

Wakan knew that from this location they could hide and still be able to see the countryside below.

Laomi and Sapa immediately curled up and slept.

Wakan kept watch, turning the events of the past few days over in his mind and wondering what the future would bring.

In the months that followed, life was lonely compared with the happiness they had experienced when Wakan and his brother and sisters were growing up. The solitary role as caretaker of his mother and sister weighed heavily on Wakan.

Laomi spent hours lamenting the loss of her mate and was not interested in hunting.

In the meantime, Wakan and Sapa searched the grassy meadows for rabbits, grouse, prairie dogs and other small game. Both felt inadequate to the task of chasing down a deer. Wakan had been on several hunts during his youth, but was never involved in leading a hunting expedition.

Wakan urged Laomi to participate in hunting, communicating through signs that he wanted to stalk some of the deer nearby.

"We must hunt to survive," Wakan urged.

Laomi only glanced at him without commenting.

The next evening, Wakan ventured into a nearby valley where he picked up the scent of deer.

Quickly he returned to the living area. Laomi was sleeping when Wakan arrived. He communicated to Laomi, "We must follow the trail, I believe there is a lame deer in the herd."

Pawing her and generating a low growl, Wakan continued to annoy his mother, forcing her to participate.

Recognizing that he was serious, Laomi got up and followed Wakan and Sapa.

The three pursued the aroma of the deer and found five of them grazing in a small secluded valley.

Laomi recognized that one of the deer, an aged buck, moved slower than the rest, obviously impaired by old injuries received in a rutting battle with a younger male.

"We will pursue this one," she conveyed to Wakan and Sapa as she looked toward the buck.

"Be careful of his antlers," she indicated.

The deer were alert to the presence of the wolves but did not run. Instead they watched intently as the small wolf family spread out in different directions, seemingly uninterested in them.

Nervously, the doe moved toward her fawns, stamping her feet and snorting. The old buck simply stood silent, watching the movements of the wolves.

The wolf family did not look directly at the game. They each glanced at the deer but acted oblivious to them.

Wakan suddenly felt an urge to stop and stare at the old buck.

The feeling came from deep within his instincts. He was not fully aware of the sensation which accompanied this urging, but he knew the impulse was driven by something deeper than he could understand.

The two animals stared at one another, unaware of the other deer or wolves.

There was a spiritual communication between the buck and Wakan.

Wakan understood that he would claim the life of this regal old animal. The message came to him through a knowledge which was already in his mind. This was instinct.

In the moments which passed, the deer also knew he would fulfill his role. He would be the sacrifice.

Wakan would be the executor.

Both understood their ancient roles of serving *nature's spirit*.

Wakan stalked the buck slowly.   Laomi and Sapa, witnessing the communications, stood on either side of the deer, ready for Wakan's signal to attack.

Wakan was first.

He attacked from the side, to avoid the buck's huge sharp antlers.

As the deer turned to defend himself from Wakan's attack, Laomi attacked from the opposite side.

Sapa leaped toward the rear legs, snapping at the tendons which would cripple the big buck.

Surprisingly, the deer began running, finding an unexpected spurt of energy. The buck led the three wolves, running at a steady pace across two miles of rugged badlands terrain.

Finally, after half an hour, the old stag turned and faced his pursuers.

Laomi approached the animal head on.   Sapa and Wakan circled around the deer on opposite sides.

Wakan was the first to leap at the deer, grabbing at the throat. His teeth tore the skin and ripped the neck muscles.

Sapa attacked the flank from the other side, slashing at the tendons.

While the buck shook his head to escape Wakan's grip, Laomi tore at the deer's mid-section, opening a gaping wound with her powerful jaws.

All three wolves inflicted fatal wounds on the deer.

In a matter of minutes, the mission was accomplished and the crippled deer was dead.

He put up a valiant fight but he knew his time had come. He died with dignity and had the respect of those who carried out the termination of his life.

This was the first of many feasts the three wolves would enjoy in the coming months.

Their hunting skills kept them well fed.

Each of the wolves felt the loss of their family but seldom communicated their loneliness.

The wolves reacted to the slaughter of their family members and the uncertainty of the fate of the others in different ways.

Sapa missed her brother and sister. She was forced to mature without the playful atmosphere she knew as a pup. She missed having family members around to play with her and teach her.

The escape to this new area was a bitter time in her young life despite the fact that she learned much from Wakan and Laomi.

Wakan also missed his family, especially his father Zando. He remembered watching the hunters drag his father's body away after the shooting. He knew the wolf he most admired and respected was gone forever.

But above all, Wakan missed Acayla.

He became increasingly aware that he had a great fondness for the attractive young female.

He had not realized the extent of his affection and that she held such a special place in his life.

He continued to believe she was still alive.

The long months of separation increased his concern and thoughts of her dominated his mind.

But it was his apprehension about Laomi that troubled Wakan most.

His mother remained despondent. She had lost her spirit, her lack of interest in even the simplest activities. Wakan knew he must do something.

He made a decision he hoped would help his mother regain her enthusiasm.

The wolves would return to their home territory in northwestern South Dakota.

The young wolf felt this might be the key to helping Laomi regain her natural function in the pack.

Also, they would find out if anyone else had survived the massacre of the previous summer.

Secretly, Wakan knew he could find his beloved Acayla and reestablish the family in the territory occupied by his ancestors. This would create a home for the generations yet to come.

CHAPTER 12

Following Zando's death, Acayla, Skola, Ohake and Nehma were pursued by hunters for two days before they finally gave up their chase. Satisfied they had run the wolves out of their territory, the ranchers returned to their homes.

Skola assumed leadership of the pack and Acayla became a strong influence in deciding where the small pack would relocate.

The wolves were now in unfamiliar territory. They followed a series of creek beds to avoid being seen by humans. After several miles, Acayla cautiously crept to the top of a hill to observe the landscape.

She saw a huge mountain in the distance, standing alone on the prairie. Fascinated by this unusual sight, Acayla returned to Skola and the others, indicating that they should go cross-country to investigate this uncommon scene. Moving silently through the tall grass, they had arrived at the old sacred Indian monument called Bear Butte.

The mountain stood like a sentinel. It was nearly as tall as the mountains of the Black Hills a few miles distant.

The group skirted the mountain and stopped at a river to rest for the day. They would look for a safe place to stay for a few days before making plans for the future.

Acayla urged her companions to hide themselves in the underbrush near the water. Then she settled into a small dugout nearby.

The wolves slept most of the day, awaking periodically to sniff the air and inspect any strange sounds they picked up.

It was during one of these waking periods that Skola moved quietly through the grass to Acayla's hiding place.

"There are other wolves nearby," he motioned.

Acayla immediately became alert and began testing the scents.

"I believe there is only one," she answered.

The two wolves moved silently along the riverbank toward the direction of the scent. They left Ohake and Nehma sleeping under a large tree, safely hidden from sight.

As Acayla and Skola approached a bend in the river, they spotted a single wolf, lapping water from the stream.

With her hair bristled, Acayla moved stiffly toward the wolf who was not yet aware of her presence.

Skola circled around behind the wolf to cut off a retreat and to prevent any surprise attack from other wolves which may have accompanied this one.

Acayla saw that this was a lone female. There were no other wolf tracks along the water's edge.

Acayla was only a few yards away when the female realized someone was approaching. She turned, pelage hairs standing on end.

The female bared her teeth and growled fiercely at Acayla, then moved slowly away from the soft sand along the river bank, to more solid footing.

Acayla also bared her teeth, but did not growl or show an aggressive nature. She looked directly into the female's eyes, attempting to intimidate her.

Skola moved out of the shadows of the tree lined riverbank just above the two wolves who stood staring at one another. Instinct cautioned him not to interfere.

The female, surprised by the arrival of the second wolf, turned and began to trot away.

"We mean you no harm," Acayla indicated as the female watched her carefully.

Skola remained silent but watchful.

"It is dangerous here," the female replied. "There are many hunters in this area and you must be careful."

Acayla offered her appreciation by ceasing the threatening snarl and lowering the pelage hairs on her shoulders.

"What is your name?" Acayla inquired.

"Noake," was the reply.

The three wolves approached one another carefully.

After a few moments, Acayla and Skola determined that the female was the lone survivor of her family which had been killed several miles south of this spot. She told them she had hidden along the river for several days, afraid to hunt or leave the shelter of the trees.

Acayla invited Noake back to the place they had been resting and suggested that the three of them attempt to find deer or other game.

Noake met Ohake and Nehma who had awakened from their naps. They had not moved from the spot where Acayla had left them.

It was late afternoon when the three adult wolves went out to find food. This was the time when deer usually left their bedding places to graze in the last warm rays of sunshine.

The three moved silently along a small creek which flowed into the river, looking in the bushes growing next to the banks, for any signs where deer had bedded down during the day.

Skola signaled that he had found such a spot and that the deer's trail was still fresh.

The group followed the tracks into a small meadow. A few minutes later, they spotted four deer grazing in the tall grass.

Using the lush growth as camouflage, the wolves stopped for only a few minutes to determine the wind direction and to plan the attack.

Acayla directed the hunt, instructing the others on where to position themselves. The trio moved slowly, crouching low to the ground, ever watchful of the movement of the deer.

The wolves stationed themselves in a triangle; surrounding one of the does grazing a short distance from the others. Acayla gave the signal to attack by standing up and leaping toward the deer.

At the same moment, Skola and Noake sprang from their positions, running at full speed toward the hoofed animal.

The doe immediately recognized her plight and jumped high in the air just as Acayla reached her. Acayla, diving for the deer's hind legs, missed and went rolling into Noake who was approaching from the other side.

Skola, still on his feet, chased the deer, but remained several steps behind, unable to catch up.

By the time Acayla and Noake regained their balance, the prey was too far away for them to attack.

The two females followed Skola in his pursuit of the animal running down the hill toward the creek. The other deer had disappeared in the opposite direction, removing themselves as targets of the predators.

When the doe reached the creek, it made a gigantic leap across and up the other side.

Moments later Skola ran down the embankment, tried to jump across to the opposite bank, but missed and slid back down. The two wolves following him had to stop to avoid running into Skola. All three stood, embarrassed, in the shallow water of the creek as the doe made her escape and disappeared from sight.

On their return to the river, the three wolves discovered a prairie dog town. The furry rodents were sitting on the edges of their holes, barking in high pitched voices alerting the community to the danger of the approaching predators.

This time Noake decided on the strategy. She instructed Skola and Acayla to distract the prairie dogs by walking around the prairie dog town in full view of the rodents. Noake, meanwhile would quietly sneak up behind the small animals and capture them.

After several attempts, the wolves managed to snatch a few of the furry creatures for their supper. Proudly the trio carried their catch back to the hideout. The three prairie dogs were barely enough to feed the five wolves but they shared the meager portions.

After the evening meal, Acayla motioned to Noake, "Are there many hunters in this area?"

"I see some nearly every day," Naoke replied.

Acayla indicated to Noake that she and the others had been attacked by hunters and that their leader, Zando, and three others had been killed. She told Noake they did not know what happened to other members of their pack.

Acayla still was not willing to believe that Wakan, Laomi and Sapa had been killed.

Noake indicated that there was an place which was fairly safe. She relayed that the area called the Black Hills was just a half day's travel from where they were.

"My family did not live in the mountains," she explained, "But we hunted there often."

Acayla and Skola agreed that Noake should join them and travel to this new territory. Another adult would also strengthen the pack, she concluded.

Early the next evening the pack of five wolves moved across the river toward the Black Hills.

In the weeks that followed, the group sharpened their hunting skills and were successful in bringing down several deer. Because the pack was so small it was necessary to accelerate the teaching of the younger members on how to help during the hunts. Soon all five wolves traveled together in search of prey.

The wolves stayed close to the foothills but as summer arrived, the days became hot and uncomfortable.

With the warming of the temperature, the hunters were increasingly active. The wolves saw riflemen closer to their hiding areas, so they decided to move to higher elevations.

The first few weeks were spent getting acquainted with their new territory. Game was fairly abundant and there was not the severe hunting pressure they had experienced on the ranches at the edge of the Black Hills.

Skola and Noake spent a great deal of time together. It was obvious to Acayla that they would mate in the spring.

Acayla was surprised that there was little wolf activity. There were not many scent marks and she saw very few signs of other packs occupying the area.

The summer passed quickly as the wolves explored the mysterious dark woods of this new territory.

Warm days and cool nights foretold the coming of Autumn. The aspen leaves had turned golden, shimmering in the bright sunlight. The pungent smell of pine filled the air as the forest prepared for colder weather.

Acayla loved the Black Hills. She especially liked to climb to the top of the rocky cliffs and look out over the vast forest.

Here, Acayla had time to think about what happened to the rest of her family. She pined over the possibility that her beloved Wakan had been killed and wondered what had happened to her friend and mentor Laomi.

Often Acayla sat on the cliff howling. It was an ideal place to sit during the evening hours. The quiet air and the rolling mountains caused her wolf songs to carry for miles.

At times she heard other wolves howl, but mostly she heard the high pitched bugle of the bull elk as their challenges echoed across the vast forest.

The pack continued to explore their territory and found deer and elk plentiful, although the task of bringing down the larger animals was a challenge for the small group.

Snows came early in the mountains. But Acayla noted that the winters were not as harsh as on the prairie and that most of the time the snow fell straight down rather than being blown into huge drifts by the prairie winds.

During the winter months, the pack had some difficulty plowing through the abundant snowfall. Often the wolves became exhausted trying to run through the deep snow.

On clear days, the temperature rose to pleasant levels, something which rarely happened during winter days on the prairie.

In late winter Noake took Skola as her mate. That spring she gave birth to six pups in a well hidden den high in the remote mountains.

Skola and Acayla continued to teach Ohake and Nehma to hunt. In addition to the deer and elk, they occasionally stalked Big Horn sheep.

Small game included marmots, grouse and wild turkeys. The turkeys offered the greatest challenge and could be approached only if they were crippled or nesting.

After the pups were about two months old, the pack moved to a rendezvous site at a lower elevation.

The pack had seen very few humans in the area, but were aware that several herds of cattle were located in their territory.

They came across more wolves as the year progressed. Other families started moving into the territories surrounding them.

At times, some wolves attacked and killed young calves. Skola was guilty of this on the occasions when the pack had not been able to capture wild game.

"Each time cattle or sheep were killed in our other home area, the hunters came and attacked us," Acayla warned. "We must not risk that again," she declared.

When these attacks became known to the ranchers, hunting parties began to track the predators. Humans did not recognize wolf territories nor did they care. Their only objective was to get rid of anything that attacked their herds.

Coyotes, which had a unquenchable taste for lamb, were nearly always involved in attacks on sheep and young calves.

Wolves, on the other hand, could bring down a full grown steer and a fairly large horse with relative ease.

Ranchers didn't care which of the species they shot, trapped or poisoned.

It was mid-summer when a lone rifleman spotted Skola lying on a hillside sunning himself. The male wolf was sleeping and unaware that danger was nearby.

The rancher took aim and shot without his victim ever being aware of what happened.

Skola's death sent a shock wave through the family. He had survived the massacre in the Slim Buttes and the one hundred mile trip to the Black Hills, only to be shot while sleeping on the hill overlooking the valley where his family was resting.

Acayla and Noake were tending to the youngsters and Ohake and Nehma were scouting in a nearby valley when the shot rang out.

"Stay with the pups," Acayla urged Noake. "I'll see what happened."

Acayla stayed in the shadows while moving toward the sound of the shot. She knew the approximate location where Skola had been resting, but as she looked on the hillside, she could not see him anywhere.

Afraid to expose herself by running into the open, Acayla stayed in the forest and sniffed the air to pick up any scents.

As she weaved in and out of the trees, she caught sight of movement ahead of her. A horse and rider were crossing the wooded valley.

The man urged his mount up the hill to where Skola was last known to have been.

Hiding in the trees, Acayla watched the man's movements. She scanned the hillside ahead of the hunter to see where he was going.

Then she spotted Skola. His head was lying at a strange angle and his body was lying half way out of a small dugout on the hillside.

The rifleman rode up to him, dismounted and walked toward the wolf.

Acayla's heart ached. She had known Skola all her life. He was two years old when she was adopted by Zando and Laomi and they had became close friends.

Skola had helped her when she had trouble learning her hunting and tracking lessons as a youngster.

Without his help during the long escape from the hunters who killed Zando and the others, she would not have been able to bring Ohake and Nehma to the safety of the Black Hills.

Skola had been enjoying his role as alpha male and delighted in his first batch of pups.

Now, his life was over.

Acayla crept away from the scene where her friend was being dragged by the rancher. She dreaded the task of informing Noake of what had happened.

Slowly Acayla returned to the place where the other wolves were resting. When she was a few yards away, she saw Noake standing near the pups, looking in her direction.

With sadness and despair, Acayla informed Noake of what had happened.

"He was lying down when the rifleman shot him," Acayla relayed.

"I doubt he knew what happened," she added, reassuringly.

Noake stood still, not moving in any direction, feeling helpless at the loss of her mate.

The pups, now three months old, were resting in the shade. Acayla nuzzled the youngsters, comforting them even though they could not realize what had happened to their father.

Acayla immediately began to look for Nehma and Ohake.

"Where are they?" she inquired.

Noake gave no sign of hearing the question.

The older female signaled Noake to lie down with her pups and keep them safe.

"I'm going to look for them," she informed the shocked mother.

Acayla found the pair walking leisurely down a deer trail. She told them of the disaster and urged them to take cover immediately. She did not know whether the rifleman was still around or if others were nearby.

For the next several weeks, Acayla took charge of everything. She organized the hunts, decided where the family would live, and generally did everything the alpha male would do.

Although her mind was constantly occupied with the care and safety of her charges, Acayla never forgot Wakan.

She never doubted that he was still alive. She was certain she saw Wakan and Laomi standing on a hill in the distance, looking down at the place where Zando and the others were killed.

That caused her to believe Wakan had escaped safely.

But here in the Black Hills, the threats against the family continued.

The first snow had fallen when Acayla's small pack came across a lone wolf. He entered their territory and approached Acayla, recognizing she was in charge.

The male was welcomed without challenge. It was obvious he was attracted to Acayla, however the female showed no interest in the male and shunned his overtures.

Finding no acceptance by Acayla, the wolf began courting Noake. He paid considerable attention to the pups and soon his interest expanded to playing with the youngsters and protecting them whenever danger was nearby.

Noake responded to the wolf's attention and together they began caring for the pups. The new wolf also took much of the responsibility of acquiring food for the pack.

This was the situation Acayla wanted. Now that Skola was dead, she decided to return to her home in the Slim Buttes and search for Wakan.

Acayla approached Ohake and Nehma, asking them if they were interested in returning to their home. Both indicated they were.

She informed the new male wolf and Noake that she and the yearlings were going to leave.

On a crisp October night, the three expressed their farewells and left.

Acayla led the two younger wolves northward following the pine covered valleys to the edge of the Black Hills.

By midnight they had reached the foothills and moved down into the prairie.

They followed creeks and valleys throughout the night, avoiding all farms and pastures.

Traveling by night and resting, well hidden in daylight, it took the trio three days to reach the southern edge of the Slim Buttes.

Happy to be back in their home territory, the wolves found a familiar rocky outcropping to spend their first day at home.

That night, Acayla and the pups began to search for scent markings of Wakan and other family members.

Several days of reconnaissance continued without success.

CHAPTER 13

Wakan, Laomi and Sapa followed the Little Missouri River southward out of the Badlands.

Wakan looked forward to seeing the familiar territory his ancestors had known for many decades.

But there was another driving force behind the decision. He wanted to find Acayla.

The exile in the Badlands lasted over a year. When he communicated his desires to Laomi and Sapa, both agreed that it was time to return home.

The small group made the trip in two days, traveling mostly at night, avoiding the watchful eyes of hunters and ranchers during the day.

When they reached the area known as the Cave Hills, they decided to stay and seek shelter in the many small caverns.

As they looked for a suitable haven, they stopped to investigate every scent marking the came across. They recognized none.

Most of the scents they found belonged to lone wolves who left their sign when passing through the area.

Wakan communicated to his mother and sister that they should stay in these hills during daylight hours and hunt on the prairie at night.

The late fall season yielded an abundance of grouse and prairie chicken and the deer population was plentiful.

As the northern winds grew colder, huge flocks of geese and ducks migrated across the territory. Periodically they landed on the small water-holes and the dwindling river pools.

Wakan was ever alert to finding the scent of Acayla, Ohake Nemah and Skola. He felt that they were still alive and hoped they were living in their old territory.

In early November, a snowstorm hit the region. The storm began at dawn with a light drizzle.

Wakan left Sapa and his mother in the rocky outcroppings of the higher hills, informing them he was going to explore and do some hunting.

Secretly, he was looking for Acayla.

As he moved eastward out of the protection of their hideout, the rain turned to sleet. By mid-afternoon, the precipitation began sticking to the blades of grass. Soon, snowflakes replaced the ice crystals.

Wakan had not discovered any game animals, but as he moved through the storm, he picked up the strong scent of a horse.

The sky was darkened by the heavy clouds, making visibility poor.

Heavy snowflakes continued to fall from the dense clouds as he followed the scent.

Shortly, he saw the figure of a man riding a horse. Wakan stayed downwind of the two creatures, but out of curiosity, followed them.

Wakan usually avoided all contact with man since the death of his father. But he found this situation unusual.

After nearly an hour, the storm turned into a heavy blizzard. The sun was now setting and darkness was only minutes away.

Still, he continued to follow the horse and rider. Wakan realized they were moving in circles. Both had apparently lost their direction in the storm and were disoriented. Wakan could see that they had crossed and recrossed their tracks in the snow.

Just before nightfall, Wakan, recognizing that the man could not find his way and could freeze to death wandering around in the storm, circled ahead of the horse and rider and stood in their path.

He waited until the horse caught his scent. Suddenly the horse stopped.

The rancher, his head tucked low inside his coat collar, looked up to see why his mount quit walking. Startled at the sight of a wolf in his path, the man reached for the rifle which he carried on the saddle.

Seeing the danger, Wakan quickly ran to the side, hidden from view by the heavy snow. In a few minutes, Wakan reappeared on the horses path.

Again the rancher raised his rifle.

Wakan moved out of sight.

After a few moments, the man urged his horse onward.

Wakan ran ahead and again moved into the path of the horse. This time, the curious rancher did not raise his rifle, but sat watching the gray wolf.

Wakan turned and walked north, looking over his shoulder to be sure the man did not threaten him again.

The rancher did not move.

Wakan stopped but stayed on the path.

The rancher waited several minutes then he prodded his horse forward.

Wakan stayed in front of the horse and rider, barely visible in the storm.

The horse was nervous at the sight and smell of a wolf and had to be commanded to continue on. After several minutes, with his head high and ears forward, the mount followed Wakan without hesitation.

Wakan guided the pair toward a fence on a nearby ranch.

The storm increased in its ferocity and at times, even though they were only a few feet behind him, Wakan could not see the horse and rider.   He sensed, however that they were still following his footprints in the snow.

After nearly two hours, Wakan came to a fence. He waited until the rancher reached the enclosure.   Then Wakan turned east and led the two along the fence line.

In about a half hour, they reached a corral and a set of buildings. Wakan knew the rancher and his mount would find shelter there.

Once the rider realized where he was, Wakan ducked through the fence and disappeared into the blizzard.

Wakan circled around behind the horse, crossed the rapidly disappearing footprints in the snow, and began his trip back to his family.

On the way back, Wakan chased and caught a large jackrabbit. He devoured the creature in a few gulps before continuing.

The blizzard did not let up throughout the entire night. Wakan fought high drifts as he made his way back to Laomi and Sapa. The snow made the countryside look different, but his sense of direction was unerring.

About midnight, the wolf arrived at the place where his mother and sister were sleeping. He caught their scent several yards away.

Wakan entered the cave, shook the snow off his coat, and found a comfortable place to lay down.

Laomi heard her son enter the enclosure but did not raise her head. Sapa rose to greet her brother, licking his face in an effort to get food.

Wakan did not oblige her but instead went to sleep, exhausted from his travels through the storm.

The next morning, the sun shown brightly on the new fallen snow.

Wakan, stiff from struggling through the snow drifts, stretched his legs in the early sunlight. His right paw was aching where he had lost his toe a year and a half before. The injury bothered him whenever he traveled great distances.

Sapa followed Wakan out of the cave.   She also stretched her legs and arched her back.

Wakan took the motion as a sign she wanted to play. He immediately jumped toward her, daring her to play a game of tag.

Sapa obliged.   The brother and sister chased one another through the snow on the hillside and rolled in the fresh powder.

The game went on for several minutes until Loami, now showing her age, came to the cave entrance and looked disapprovingly at the two wolves thrashing in the snow below her.

She did not join in their frolicking and instead, lay down to observe the countryside.

In a few minutes Wakan and Sapa tired of their game and came back where Laomi lay quietly. She had dozed off while waiting for her youngsters.

Laomi still did not take a great deal of interest in anything.

Wakan tried to keep her involved in hunting since it was very difficult for two wolves to get enough food to sustain the group.

Without Laomi's help, Wakan and Sapa learned several tricks to hunting and managed to kill several deer by attacking the animal from both front and back at the same time.

This morning, they would try again. Wakan knew that Laomi and Sapa had not eaten for several days and his only nourishment was the jackrabbit he caught the night before.

Wakan led Sapa to a valley below the hills. As the pair crossed the head of a washout, Wakan noticed some movement down inside the ditch.

He stopped and observed before moving forward, not wanting to expose himself or his sister to any possible danger.

As they approached the washout, they noticed the activity came from a yearling antelope which was caught belly deep in a snowdrift.

It was apparent the animal had tried to cross the washout during the blizzard and became bogged down in the snow. The animal could not gain footing and lay helpless. The antelope had struggled for several hours and with each movement sank deeper into the drift.

Now, nearly exhausted, the pronghorn waited for certain death.

Wakan and Sapa obliged.

The two wolves stepped carefully onto the snow piled around the pronghorn. Their broad feet kept them from sinking too deeply into the drift.

Wakan steadied himself, then lunged at the back of the pronghorn's neck. He bit hard into the spine just below the animal's head.

A loud snap indicated that he had broken the animals vertebrae. The pronghorn's body went limp.

Sapa immediately began digging the snow away from the side of the antelope. In a few minutes, she cleared enough away to tear open its side.

Hungrily, she bit into the flesh without regard to any thought of which of them should eat first.

Wakan, smelling the fresh blood and realizing he was also extremely hungry, began biting into the rump of the animal.

After an hour of eating their fill, both wolves backed out of the snow-covered ditch, stomachs gorged. They immediately turned toward the cave where Laomi lay waiting.

When Laomi saw the pair coming up the hill, she realized they had just eaten. She ran down the slope to greet them, begging for regurgitated food. Both of her pups obliged.

The wolves visited the pronghorn's carcass every few hours, making sure that the valuable meat was preserved. They took large portions and stored it near their cave.

On one visit to the carcass, Wakan surprised three coyotes that had discovered the meat and were feasting.

Wakan had very little regard for his yellow cousins and showed his authority by attacking all three as he approached his prize.

The coyotes, equally as hungry as the wolves, stood their ground. But the challenge lasted only a few moments as Wakan lashed out at the closest coyote. Baring his teeth and biting fiercely, Wakan tore the skin of the coyote.

Yelping with his tail between his legs, the coyote retreated. Wakan's growling and the coyote's cries disheartened the other two animals and they followed their brother into the snow.

Wakan, not particularly hungry, checked around the carcass for any scent or tracks of man.

Satisfied that none were there, he ate a few bites of meat, then found a comfortable place to lie down.

The coyotes scampered to a nearby hill and sat watching the wolf.

Wakan knew they were waiting for him to leave, so he settled in and spent several hours there, denying the coyotes any chance of a free dinner.

Late in the afternoon, the coyotes gave up the vigil and disappeared.

Wakan tore a front leg and shoulder from the carcass and carried it back to the cave for his mother and sister.

The small family felt good about being back in familiar territory and decided that night, they would explore the area to the south.

Making sure the cached food was safe, Wakan entered the small cave and rested until nightfall.

CHAPTER 14

When darkness came, Laomi was restless and indicated she wanted to accompany Wakan and Sapa.

Since she had eaten her fill of fresh meat from the pronghorn, Laomi regained much of her energy and was ready to move on.

Wakan led the two females southeast toward the Slim Buttes. The trip took several hours and Laomi seemed to regain her energy as they approached the ridge of the buttes they called home.

The strong northerly winds during the blizzard deposited huge drifts on the south side of the buttes. The wolves stayed on the top of the hills where the snow had blown clear and the traveling was easier.

Passing through a familiar area, Wakan remembered that this was where Zando led the pack nearly two years ago, searching for safety from the hunters and trappers.

The place brought back memories of when he and his litter-mates played with the other members of the pack.

He thought of Acayla and how she had taken care of him and saw to it he always had plenty of food.

As the wolves moved silently through the trees, Wakan suddenly stopped. He recognized a familiar scent.

Searching the vicinity, he found several urine markings, proof that other wolves were nearby.

"Something is familiar about this scent," Wakan related to Laomi.

The old female approached and sniffed.

"It's Acayla," she declared.

Wakan felt a wave of relief and happiness.

"She's alive," he announced.

Wakan immediately began searching for tracks. Excited about seeing Acayla, the young male ran quickly from scent marking to scent marking, trying to find the freshest one.

Frustrated, Wakan broke the silence the pack had maintained since returning to the area. He lifted his head and howled.

He repeated his mournful cry several times. Laomi and Sapa joined in.

After a few minutes, the three stood silently waiting for a reply.

They waited only a few seconds. A howl echoed through the hills. Then another, and another.

The sounds were nearby.

Excited, Wakan ran toward the sound of the voices, his mother and sister followed closely.

Every few seconds Wakan stopped and howled. The answers came quickly. They were closer now.

The distance between the wolves narrowed.

As Wakan cut across a small valley, he spotted Acayla and his brother and sister coming down a wooded hillside.

Wakan rushed to meet Acayla.

The two wolves approached one another, smiling, whining, tails straight in the air wagging furiously.

Suddenly all six wolves were together, licking, nuzzling, jumping up on one another, rolling in the snow and playing games of tag.

It was a joyous reunion.

Each wolf expressed their happiness, mischievously nipping at each other's tails and mouths.

There was no thought given to rank or authority, this was an occasion for celebrating.

The frolicking lasted throughout the night. Yipping, barking and growling was punctuated with choruses of howls.

The family was back together again.

From that moment on, Wakan and Acayla became constant companions. Both matured physically during the time they were apart, and now the affection which had developed while they were youngsters turned to love.

Wakan and Acayla became the unchallenged alpha pair. There was no disagreement in this close-knit family, and Nehma, the only other male, deferred to Wakan's authority in all things. As for Wakan's sisters, there was no question in their minds about Acayla becoming the alpha female.

The family quickly became a thriving unit again. Under Wakan's leadership, they re-established their territory and conducted successful hunting expeditions regularly.

Still they avoided contact with the ranchers and homesteaders in the area. The wild game was plentiful and none of the wolves particularly liked to eat the flesh of domestic livestock.

Even Laomi regained her enthusiasm. She began again to teach her youngsters to develop their talents and expertise.

Nehma became an excellent hunter. He, Wakan and Acayla often teamed up to bring down deer and pronghorn, keeping the herds clear of the diseased and weak, allowing nature to help strengthen the game herds.

Sapa and Ohake helped with hunting when necessary and always took care of their aging mother Laomi.

Wakan did not realize how much he missed Acayla until he had to spend the year separated from her. He had thought about her every day they were apart.

For Acayla, the splitting up of the pack gave her time to realize that she wanted to be Wakan's mate. During the time she was in the Black Hills Acayla concluded that she must find her special companion.

The two spent nearly every hour together throughout the rest of the winter. In February, when Acayla came into heat, they became lovers and spent hours caressing and mating. They were devoted to each other and determined to make their pack strong again.

The family stayed mainly in the Slim Buttes, spending most of their time together in the beautiful haven among the evergreens.

The ranchers in the area were aware that wolves had returned because of the nightly howling. Again the wolves became the focus of increased hunting and trapping activities. Wakan urged his pack to stay out of sight of the humans.

As spring approached and the weather warmed, Laomi became even more active.

As Acayla's whelping time approached, Laomi communicated to Wakan and his mate that she would select the den where the pups would be born.

In the weeks that followed, several den sites were scouted, but none proved suitable. Finally, in mid-April, Laomi led the small family several miles west, back to the Little Missouri River, the area where she had given birth to Wakan, Sapa, Ohake and Nehma.

"I want you to use the same den I used for my first batch of pups," Laomi announced to Acayla.

"I remember finding that den," Acayla boasted. "I hope we can locate it."

The small river had changed very little since they left. When Zando was still alive the pack hunted the abundant herds of deer along portions of the river.

Laomi took pride in leading the family back to the region, traveling mainly at night and hunting along the way. There were a few scent markings left by individual wolves, but there wasn't a pattern designating another pack's territory.

When the family arrived they immediately began searching for familiar landmarks.

After exploring most of the day, Laomi was not able to find the location. Acayla could remember only the large cottonwood trees above the den, but little else came to her memory.

Late in the day, Wakan brought the pack together and insisted that they rest for the night and continue the search.

Early the next morning, Laomi and Acayla left the pack and proceeded along the bottomlands near the river. The spring runoff from the snow-covered hills, made the water too deep for them to follow the riverbank.

About an hour later, Acayla indicated, "There it is."

Laomi rushed to the entrance, still hidden just above the rushing water in the side of the riverbank.

"It's still here," she motioned as the older wolf entered the den.

Acayla was excited about the discovery. The two females explored the enclosure. "Nothing has changed," Laomi proclaimed.

"I'll get Wakan," Acayla conveyed as she left the matriarch to relive her memories of this important place.

"We found it," Acayla signaled to her mate. "It hasn't changed at all," she added.

Wakan and the others followed Acayla along the five mile distance to the den.

Ohake and Sapa traded excited barks as they approached the huge trees. Both faintly remembered the area.

Nehma recalled the spring and summer months the family spent playing in the shade of the trees and underbrush along the river.

The sight of the den brought other memories to Wakan. He remembered the times he had spent with his father Zando and the many lessons the older wolf had taught him.

For the next several days, the family explored and played often recalling events of their childhood.

Sapa found the place where she and Wakan had jumped into the swift water while chasing ducks. Ohake and Nehma reminisced about playing hide-and-seek among the cattails along the riverbank.

Soon, the time for Acayla to have her pups approached. Wakan was continuously by her side. Laomi helped the young female prepare the den.

Finally, Sapa convinced Wakan to accompany the rest of the family to track down some game and cache meat for Acayla.

The two sisters and two brothers left Acayla and Laomi in the den and went hunting. It had been a long time since the four of them had spent so much time together.

They worked as a well-trained team, capturing two older buck deer and feasting on their carcasses. After eating their fill, they carried large chunks of meat back to the den for Acayla and Laomi to eat, and some to store away.

Laomi was beginning to lose her strong teeth and was no longer able to tear her food from the big chunks. The wolves saw to it that their mother was fed with the partially digested food they regurgitated.

The next day, Acayla retreated into the den. The spring flowers were just beginning to bloom on the prairie and the warm spring weather was delightful.

Wakan nervously watched over the entrance. He paced back and forth and would not be comforted.

After the first night, Wakan looked inside the den. He heard his mate growl softly and listened for the sounds of pups. Hearing none, he backed out and resumed his anxious watch.

Later in the day, Laomi entered to check on the young female. Acayla allowed her inside and she discovered that the young female had given birth to six pups, all healthy and lively.

Laomi came outside and motioned to Wakan. The young alpha male quickly responded to his mother's signal. She broke the news to the patiently waiting family.

Wakan experienced a feeling of fulfillment. He was now able to continue the legacy of his father and the generations before him. "This family will live on," he proclaimed.

The small family rejoiced by playing games and howling throughout the night.

Each member took their turn bringing fresh meat to Acayla, snatching brief looks at the batch of newborns.

Ten days after they were born, Acayla brought the youngsters to the entrance of the den. It was a happy day for Wakan. He had lost patience waiting for the pups to mature enough to join in family activities.

Daily, Acayla escorted her litter outside.

Wakan, the proud father, played for hours with the bundles of fur, showing equal affection to each one.

The spring passed quickly and the pups grew more active with each passing day.

In early summer, the pack began hunting deer on the prairie following the animals as they moved around looking for fresh new grass.

Three weeks after the pups were born, Wakan and Acayla proudly announced the names of their babies.

They named the first son Sapir. He was a large black pup, who was the same color as his grandfather Zando.

The other sons were Topa and Ozhe, both had dark gray coats similar to their father. The three female pups were named Naza, Caldra and Okazaki. All three females were light gray like their mother.

The family was now double in size. By mid-summer they moved to a rendezvous site near the mouth of a spring-fed creek.

On a bright and cheerful afternoon, Acayla proudly took her new brood exploring. The youngsters played in the new grass and soaked in the warm rays from the sun.

The pups were fat and furry and moved clumsily as they chased each other in a seemingly endless game of tag.

Acayla was momentarily distracted while watching four of the pups wrestle with a bone they found. Amused at the sight, she failed to see a huge bald eagle swoop down on Okazaki, picking up the youngster with his lethal talons.

Before Acalya could react, the eagle swept into the sky, wings pounding the quiet spring air.

Acayla was helpless. She stood by and watched as the gigantic bird flew away with her offspring.

In shock, the alpha female gathered the remaining five pups and herded them back to the nearby trees for protection.

After the brood was safely hidden, Acayla barked an alarm to the rest of the family.

Wakan ran to his mate's side, then counted the youngsters. Acayla explained to Wakan what had happened, but she was unable to describe the incident clearly.

Wakan knew that Okazaki was gone and that there was no need to look for the pup.

The incident caused Acayla and Wakan to closely watch over the remainder of their family.

The couple saw to it that if they were to be gone from the pups, that other members of the family took over the duties.

Wakan paid close attention to his family and often volunteered to baby-sit the youngsters, allowing Acayla time to exercise and hunt.

As his family matured, Wakan gained confidence as a leader. He knew he was restoring his ancestors legacy. He remembered the lessons he had learned about leadership and preserving the family unit. He often thought of Zando, an example of the role of wolves in nature.

Wakan combined the knowledge of his heritage with the recent experiences in dealing with humans. He vowed to teach his own offspring about their function in nature, and emphasize that they cannot trust man.

The young alpha wolf developed a plan to avoid coming in contact with humans on a regular basis.

Since he noticed that the number of wolf packs had declined since his father's death, he decided to explore all the surrounding territory and expand his family's domain. A larger area would offer greater opportunity to hunt without conflict with ranchers, and would lessen the need to kill domestic animals in order to survive.

But Wakan would soon find out that even in the two years since Zando had been killed and that the pack had been away from the locale, additional homesteaders had moved in.

That meant more ranches, more cattle, more sheep, fewer deer, pronghorn, and other wildlife.

Nevertheless, Wakan staked out a territory much larger than any of his ancestors had ever claimed. When the pups were old enough to travel, he scent marked a domain nearly a hundred miles long and seventy miles wide.

Wakan knew that in order to survive, he must keep his family on the move. He recognized that his father's mistake was not moving around enough. By staying in their smaller territory, Zando had unwittingly provided an opportunity for the ranchers and hunters to track the family and keep hunting pressure on them.

During his young life, Wakan tried to figure out why wolves stayed within their marked territories, while ranchers did not follow the same rules.

He felt the wolves scent-marked areas were similar to the fences built by humans.

He could not understand why the ranchers regularly went beyond these lines to pursue the wolves and other game. This was a lesson the entire pack needed to learn. Due to the human's lack of respect for territorial boundaries, wolves were not safe anywhere.

The generations of Wakan's ancestors instilled in their offspring the knowledge that wolves had few adversaries. For centuries, wolves lived near Indians and Eskimos who seldom threatened their existence.

Indians and Eskimos lived off the land, killing only when necessary, and wasting nothing.

So did wolves.

Indians and Eskimos respected nature and used their knowledge of the environment and their fellow animals to survive.

So did wolves.

Indians and Eskimos had fierce loyalty to their families and to the tribe.

So did wolves.

Indian and Eskimo tribes held the wolf in such high regard that many prayed to the *Great Spirit* to make them like the wolf, and that they be given the ability to imitate the wolf's stamina and stoicism.

Through the centuries, the relationship between these civilizations grew.

Many Medicine Men studied wolves' habits and used the language of these animals in their ceremonies.

Shaman's used wolf hides and skulls as a part of their healing rituals and used wolf signs and mannerisms when treating wounded or dying members of their tribes.

Wakan was aware that these native humans patterned their hunting techniques after the wolf. Caching food for future use and communicating with their prey, were a part of the lessons Indians learned by observing wolves.

But the white men, who built farms and ranches in territories occupied by wolves for centuries, did not understand or appreciate these qualities.

Their fears and hatreds were obvious in their attempt to eradicate wolves from the entire country.

This had been on going for several years, and intensified during Wakan's lifetime.

No matter where Wakan's family and the other wolf packs claimed a territory, the white men pursued them, shooting, trapping, poisoning, and digging out their newborn pups from their dens.

The pattern of life was changing dramatically and Wakan hoped that his plan of expanding their territory would be a solution.

Another problem plagued the wolves. Wildlife, which was abundant when the Indians lived in the area, was now rapidly disappearing.

In Wakan's memory he knew that millions of buffalo roamed the plains during his great-grandfather's time. Elk had also lived in the area during his grandfather's time, and ample numbers of deer and other animals lived there when his father was still alive.

But that was changing now. Often the only food available to the wolves was the farmer's and rancher's domestic livestock.

For the wolves, this created a serious dilemma. The homesteaders hunted or drove wildlife out of the area. These animals were the livelihood for Wakan's family.

In order to survive, the wolves frequently harvested their meat from the cattle and sheep that replaced wildlife. When they did, the humans took revenge against them.

Wakan was born into an era when wolves could not survive in the same manner they had experienced for thousands of years.

He realized that their way of life was threatened. Their very existence was in jeopardy.

He did not fully understand why, but Wakan felt a determination to restore what had been for centuries the wolf's heritage.

CHAPTER 15

When Acayla gave birth to her second litter of pups, the spring weather was clear and sunny.

This batch was born near the Grand River, about a hundred miles northeast of the Slim Buttes.

Wakan's plan to expand the family's territory brought the pack to these environs.

These were rolling hills covered with gumbo grass and less sage brush than in the west.

Since mid-winter, the ranchers, hunters and professional trappers had harassed the wolf pack almost daily.

The winter's heavy snow cover made it easy for trackers to follow their trails as the wolf pack searched for food each day.

Wild game was scarce and traps and poisoned carcasses were everywhere.

Every member of the family had experienced being shot at or chased by hunters with dogs.

Despite the hunting pressure, Wakan and Acayla mated. She came into heat a little later than normal and copulation came in March.

The pups were born in early May and the parents had to continually move them.

Again, Wakan was proud of his new brood. However, he had little time to spend playing with these offspring. Tension ran high in the pack and the wolves used every trick they could imagine to lead hunters away from the den and the places where the family congregated.

Hunting success was sporadic. There were times, while Acayla was in the den with the pups, that other members of the pack brought her meat. She did not question its origin, but knew that some members of the pack had killed livestock in order to survive.

The first time they were forced to move came two weeks after the pups were born.

Riders came to within a few feet of the den entrance. All the wolves were hidden and Acayla stayed inside, nursing the pups to keep them from making noise.

The hunters saw several wolf tracks, but could not find any signs leading to the entrance to the den. After about an hour of searching, the men moved away from the area.

Everyone in the family was afraid they would not be as lucky if the hunters returned.

"It is time to move on," Acayla indicated as she met Wakan just outside the den.

"Yes, it is too dangerous here," he replied.

Laomi approached, signalling silently, "I have found another den for you and the pups. We must move them quickly," she noted.

Acayla trusted Laomi's judgement.

She entered the den and brought out one of the pups and laid it at Wakan's feet.

Then she returned with another for Laomi.

Laomi and her son waited for the young mother to return with the third baby.

When Acayla emerged from the den, she set the pup down gently and signaled to Sapa to stay inside the den with the remaining three puppies.

Sapa obeyed.

Then Laomi led Wakan and Acayla, each gripping the skin on the back of a pup's neck. The babies whimpered softly but did not struggle. Acayla motioned to the five yearlings to follow.

As the others left with the pups, Ohake and Nehma departed to try their luck hunting.

Nehma had picked up the scent of deer about sunset. He took his sister to explore their whereabouts.

The luster of a bright moon gave Laomi, Acayla and Wakan ample light to see their way across the prairie.

As Laomi and Acayla walked ahead of Wakan, he saw the moonlight glistening off his mate's back. She was becoming more beautiful as she matured and Wakan's affection toward her increased.

The trio approached the new den site. It was more than two miles away, hidden deep in a canyon overgrown with bushes and scrub oak.

Wakan and Acayla stopped at the rim of the gorge, waiting for the family to catch up.

Laomi led the family down the side of the canyon through the heavy growth. It became increasingly dark as they descended.

"This is ideal," Wakan thought. "The hunters cannot ride their horses through this growth."

When they arrived at a small depression on the side of the canyon, Laomi indicated, "This is it."

Acayla took a moment to let her eyes adjust.

"This is an excellent place to hide the pups," she exclaimed.

Wakan communicated, "I will dig the debris out of cave while you and Laomi go back for the other three pups."

Acayla agreed as she turned to follow Laomi out of the dark canyon.

Wakan noticed the new den was much smaller than the one they had just left.

"It will have to do," he thought.

He dug away the dirt and small stones inside the shallow depression, tunneling his way back to give his mate more room. At the same time he kept a watchful eye on the three sleepy pups huddled together in the chilly night air.

The yearlings explored the area around the new den.

"Don't stray too far," Wakan warned.

The pups obeyed.

"Acayla will have to lay across the entrance to keep the pups from tumbling out," he thought as he continued to dig.

Meanwhile Acayla and Laomi traveled the distance between the two dens in a matter of minutes.

"Sapa will have to come back with us to carry the third pup," Acayla indicated to Laomi.

"Once we get them all in the new den, Sapa and Wakan can help Ohake and Nehma hunt, " she added.

Laomi nodded in agreement. "I will watch the pups and the yearlings while you finish the den," the alpha wolf offered.

The final move took only a half-hour as the females moved through the darkness, each carrying a pup in their lightly clinched teeth.

When they arrived at the new den, Acayla informed Wakan that he and Sapa no longer needed to stay.

She nuzzled her mate affectionately, thanking him for getting the den ready.

Wakan and his sister left the dense growth of the canyon and crossed the prairie in the moonlight looking for Ohake and Nehma.

At the edge of a large pasture, both sniffed the air in an attempt to pick up the scents of their brother and sister.

"We cannot howl this close to the den," Wakan warned. "If there are hunters out tonight, we could be putting the rest of the family in danger."

Sapa nodded.

Wakan knew where the other two wolves planned to hunt and led Sapa to a ridge overlooking the pasture where the ranchers kept their sheep.

"We need to find food tonight," Wakan indicated.

Sapa replied, "It's been several days since we've had fresh meat."

Just then, Sapa picked up the scent of her siblings. "They went this way," she communicated to Wakan.

He turned and followed her lead.

A few hundred yards down the hill, they met their brother and sister.

"Several deer are grazing in the pasture," Nehma gestured.

"We must be very careful in our approach," Wakan warned.

The four wolves easily jumped the woven wire fence that enclosed the sheep.

They had no difficulty following the scent of the deer.

As they approached the small herd, Wakan instructed the others. "We can spread out and circle them. Look for old or crippled ones."

But there were no weak or aged members in the herd.

Sapa and Ohake selected a yearling doe and started to chase it toward Wakan and Nehma. The deer, alert to the presence of all four wolves, turned sharply and followed the remainder of the herd, which were spooked when the wolves revealed themselves.

There was no opportunity for surprise and the deer quickly outdistanced the wolves after only a mile chase.

"We cannot run them down," Sapa declared as she quit running.

Wakan and Ohake also slowed their pace.

Nehma continued to follow, then turned aside. He spotted a band of sheep a short distance away.

In his frustration over the hunting failure, Nehma moved into the flock. His assault on the sheep was brief. He killed two in rapid succession.

Wakan led the others to the area looking for their brother. They spotted him as he ripped open the hind quarters of the larger of the two sheep.

"This is dangerous," Wakan warned.

"We must take food back to Acayla and Laomi," Nehma argued.

Wakan did not disagree.

All four wolves rapidly ate their fill. With their stomachs bulging, they headed back across the pasture, over the fence, and straight to the safety of the deep canyon.

The sun began to lighten up the eastern sky as the pack returned to the washouts leading to the canyon.

Laomi, Acayla and the yearlings eagerly greeted the four, returning wolves.

After providing food for them, the wolves found a comfortable place to lie down and rest from the night's activities.

Wakan related the experiences of the hunt to his mate and his mother.

"The deer escaped," he indicated. "Nehma killed two sheep so there will be enough food for a few days."

Their hunger satisfied, Acayla returned to the den to feed her pups.

Early the next morning, a lone rider surveyed the carcasses in the pasture.

The man dismounted from his horse and inspected the tracks around the dead sheep.

"Three Toes!" he shouted as he observed the wolf footprints on the ground near the dead animals.

"That damn renegade is going to get it," he swore.

The hunter spread a small tarp around the sheep and knelt down on it. Then he opened a bottle he carried in his coat pocket and liberally applied a substance on the flesh of both animals.

"They'll be surprised when they come back to eat here again," he muttered to himself.

The rider was confident that the nearly odorless poison would not be noticed by the dining wolves until it was too late.

"I'll get him this time," the rancher vowed as he stepped off the tarp, refolded it and mounted his horse. The rancher rode away leaving the carcasses undisturbed.

CHAPTER 16

Nehma indicated to Wakan that he wanted to take one of the yearling pups out of the canyon to explore the territory.

Wakan responded, admonishing his younger brother to be careful to watch for signs of humans, and to check every trail for traps.

Nehma chose a yearling male named Ozhe.

The two wolves headed along the river to investigate the game trails and to spot animals they would stalk later in the night when the rest of the pack would join them.

After traveling about three miles, the pair picked up the scent of deer. The trail took them south across open prairie until they reached a fence line.

The scent became stronger and Nehma wanted to locate the prey before returning to the canyon to alert the others. He counted on the deer staying in the same location to graze after dark.

While following the trail, the two wolves passed the area where Nehma had killed the sheep the night before.

He led Ozhe to the site where the carcasses lay. Nehma warned Ozhe to stay while he looked around the two sheep. He did not see any sign that they had been disturbed. He failed to see the horse hoof prints nearby.

Nehma sniffed the carcasses, but picked up no human scents. He motioned to Ozhe to join him in eating.

After only a few bites, Ozhe began shaking his head violently. Nehma stopped eating long enough to watch him. The yearling pup backed away from the carcass and began rolling on the ground. He then stood up and shook his entire body.

Nehma tore off another piece of meat from the area of the carcass where Ozhe had been eating. He stood chewing the meat while eyeing his nephew's antics, unable to figure out what was happening.

Suddenly, Nehma felt a burning in his mouth. He gagged and tried to spit out the meat he had just eaten. His throat tightened as he tried to expel the food, but it did no good.

Soon both wolves were writhing in pain at the feet of the two sheep, neither able to help the other.

Ozhe regained his senses for a moment and began running toward the fence in the direction of their new home. He made it only a few yards before his back legs stiffened and he was unable to stand up.

Nehma continued to roll on the ground, legs kicking in the air. The terrible pain overpowered him and he burst forth with a loud barking growl which turned into a high pitched scream.

Ozhe lost consciousness moments after hearing the cries of the older wolf. He died minutes later.

Nehma scratched the ground with his legs, trying to get to his feet. He desperately wanted a drink of water to wash the awful taste from his mouth and throat.

Cramps began attacking his stomach and he curled up in a tight ball in an attempt to ease the pain.

Nothing helped.

Within a half hour Nehma lost consciousness. His breathing was sporadic as he gasped for air.

When darkness settled across the canyon, Wakan inquired as to whether Acayla wanted to accompany him on the night's hunt.

"Laomi will take care of the puppies," she replied as she looked forward to her first hunting expedition since they were born.

Sapa and two of the other yearling pups, Topa and Sapir, joined the alpha pair as they left the canyon.

Laomi entered the den and comforted the six pups who were missing their mother. Ohake and the other yearling named Newah stayed to keep the old female company.

Wakan led the group along the same path that had been taken by Nehma and Ozhe earlier in the evening. Their scent was still strong. The family was carefree as they moved along the trail, since there was no sign of game or humans in that area.

When the group approached the river bend where Nehma picked up the scent of deer, Wakan stopped. He signaled the others to wait until he investigated.

Moments later, Wakan signaled, "They are following deer."

The alpha wolf could detect the scents of both Nehma and the deer.

The pack moved on in pursuit of fresh meat.

When they reached the fence, Wakan moved more cautiously. He was always alert to the possibility that humans could be lurking anywhere inside the enclosure which held their livestock.

He continued to detect the scents of the deer and the two wolves.

Wakan recognized the vicinity where they had chased deer the night before, realizing that it was near the place where Nehma killed the two sheep.

The alpha male stopped.

He signaled to Acayla, "Nehma and Ozhe turned here, but the deer trail continues on."

Puzzled by the change in direction, Wakan cautiously followed the scent of the wolves. Acayla and the rest of the pack waited a few moments, then walked slowly in their leader's footsteps.

It was cloudy and there was no moonlight to illuminate the trail ahead.

Wakan sensed that something was not right as he approached the location where the slaughter had taken place the night before.

He saw the outlines of the two sheep, their white woolly coats standing out in the darkness.

Wakan was so intent on watching for human signs that he did not notice Nehma's body until he was close to the sheep. Then he spotted his brother. The alpha wolf turned and stood across the trail in front of the others, ordering them to not go further.

Acayla approached Wakan, looking beyond her mate. She saw Nehma and rushed by the alpha male and moved warily toward the immobile form in the grass.

Wakan ordered the rest of the pack to remain motionless. "Do not move," he instructed. "Lie down in the grass and don't raise your heads until I tell you."

Then he followed Acayla as she approached Nehma.

"He's still breathing," she said as she sniffed around his head.

Wakan circled Nehma's body, looking for clues as to what had happened. Noting that there were no traps or bullet wounds, he guessed that the wolf had been poisoned.

"Acayla," he warned, "do not lick his mouth or touch the meat next to his body."

The alpha female nudged her brother-in law, but he did not move.

As Wakan and Acayla stood over Nehma, they witnessed his last sigh. His breathing stopped.

Wakan stood for a long moment over his brother's body.

Sensing that he wanted to be alone with Nehma, Acayla nuzzled her mate gently and turned back toward the other wolves, who were patiently waiting in the grass.

"Nehma is dead," she signaled to Sapa.

The dead wolf's sister emitted a low whine but did not move from her place.

Acayla laid down beside the grief stricken female with her head across the back of Sapa's neck. There they waited for Wakan to return to the pack.

In the grief and trauma of finding Nehma dying, Acayla thought about her son Ozhe.

As she lay comforting Sapa, she assumed that he must have left the area when Nehma was stricken and returned directly to the canyon.

In a few moments, Wakan returned.

"Where is Ozhe?" he inquired, asking no one in particular.

"Maybe he returned to the canyon," Acayla replied.

Wakan instructed the entire family that they should not go near the sheep carcasses.

"There is poison there," he indicated.

"We must be careful, the humans may have also set traps," he added.

As the group reassembled to leave, Acayla caught the scent of her son Ozhe.

"I know he's here," she motioned to Wakan.

The alpha wolf joined his wife, rubbing his head on her side. "We'll look together," he signaled.

Wakan instructed Sapa to take the yearlings back to the fence they had crossed just minutes before.

"Stay next to the fence and do not move around too much," he indicated.

Sapa led the youngsters away.

Meanwhile Acayla began making a wide circle around the carcasses trying to pick up Ozhe's scent.

Wakan moved in a circle in the opposite direction, sniffing the ground.

Near the sheep, he picked up the younger wolf's scent. It seemed to cover a wide area. Then he noticed scratches in the dirt and a trail leading away from the carcasses. He followed.

Within a few yards, he saw his son's body, quietly lying curled up as if sleeping.

He approached the young wolf, sniffing carefully.

Ozhe was dead.

Wakan, standing over his son's body, looked to the sky and howled mournfully.

Acayla, shocked by the sudden howl, stopped. She knew that Wakan had found Ozhe.

The alpha female ran toward the mournful sound, disregarding any thought of traps.

She approached Ozhe's body and tried to move it with her muzzle.

Then both Wakan and Acayla lay down beside the body, sadly looking at the lifeless form.

The scene did not change for more than an hour. The grief stricken parents curled next to their yearling pup until his body became cold and stiff.

Finally, Wakan arose and nudged Acayla to her feet. "It's time to go," he gestured.

The mother stood for a moment taking one last look. Then Wakan led his mate from the tragic scene, back to the living.

At the fence, no one needed a signal about what Wakan and Acayla had found.

Silently, the pack returned across the prairie in single file, their heads lowered.

When they reached the canyon edge, Ohake, Topa and Sapir were waiting. They heard their father's howls and realized something had happened.

Together the family entered the canyon.

Wakan was not looking forward to breaking the news to his mother. She had suffered so much grief at the loss of other family members, he knew it would torment her to know her son and grandson were dead.

CHAPTER 17

Wakan, Acayla and Laomi mourned the death of Nehma and Ozhe for several days.

Their sorrow was displayed in their extended howling bouts and their lack of interest in hunting or any of the other family activities.

Laomi's grief was severe, she had never really gotten over the loss of her mate Zando and three of her children.

Wakan had experienced anguish at the loss of the family members, including his father, but the death of his brother and son changed his outlook dramatically. He brooded over these deaths and became angry and difficult to be around.

Acayla mourned deeply but was more even-tempered than Wakan. Her solid character helped her through this difficult time, but she was intensely shaken by the losses.

She occupied herself with the pups, doting over them, alert to their every move. She became overly indulgent and worried constantly about them.

This concern also overflowed to her older batch of pups. The remaining four: Topa, Sapir, Newah and Caldra, were anxious to accompany Ohake and Sapa on hunting trips. Acayla, however kept a close eye on their activities and cautioned them whenever they ventured away from the site of the den.

The death of Nehma left Wakan as the only adult male in the pack. While he was alive, Nehma had always aided in leadership as the beta male. But now, Wakan had to teach young Topa and Sapir to assist him.

The alpha male remembered his own experiences after Zando had been killed. He had to assume the role of leader to help his mother and sister survive during their exile in the Badlands.

To help him forget the catastrophe involving Nehma and Ozhe, Wakan occupied his time by teaching Topa and Sapir. He also relied on Sapa to help him teach the youngsters.

The two older wolves included lessons about how to detect traps and poison.

While teaching, Wakan became an expert.

He developed his sense of smell to the extent that he could easily detect the almost odorless strychnine. Few poison settings escaped his detection.

The lessons would go on for hours. The four animals stalked rabbits, grouse, deer and pronghorn nearly every day. Other game attracted their notice as the season progressed. Ducks and geese were beginning their migration, often landing on the river nearby or in small lakes.

Wakan noted that Sapir was the most aggressive pup. He reminded the alpha male of himself at that age, constantly venturing out and exploring, willing to attempt anything.

Wakan chose the pack's hunting routes judiciously. He avoided fenced-in areas and stayed away from all dead animals in the vicinity.

He continually cautioned his family to not approach a carcass unless the pack had just killed the animal.

Often the pack noticed human activity, but in the weeks that followed the poisoning of Nehma and Ozhe, there were no life-threatening incidents.

When the alpha male was not training his youngsters, he spent his time with Acayla.

Laomi stayed close to the den, too old to hunt with the rest of the family, but was still able to tend the youngsters.

Acayla took advantage of the freedom to be with her mate.

The two wolves avoided any reference to the loss of their son, but it was constantly on their minds. Now they better understood the agony and despair felt by Zando and Laomi when their offspring had been slaughtered.

The two affectionate mates grew closer as the summer and autumn seasons passed.

The pups were maturing and the parents spent nearly all of their waking hours playing with the youngsters, making sure they were safe and secure.

Instead of moving away from the den as they normally would have done when the pups were a couple months old, the family stayed in the canyon. Wakan constantly reminded the family to find alternate entrances and to remain alert to the danger of being tracked by dogs. It was because of these precautions that the canyon continued to be a safe haven. Even after all these months, the ranchers had not discovered the hiding place of the wolf pack.

Once Wakan and Acayla decided the new pups were old enough to travel, they took the pack out of the canyon and headed south toward the Moreau River.

They were moving to a new territory because Wakan was fearful that man's hunting activity would increase as winter approached. He believed their luck would not hold out in their present location.

On a foggy, damp morning in early October, Wakan led his family away from the Grand River. This had been their home for nearly a year, but this, like most other places they traveled, held sad memories of lost family members.

Wakan's keen sense of direction took the family through some areas recently settled by ranchers and farmers. He avoided homesteads, and steered his group away from the huge herds of sheep which dotted the hillsides.

There were more sheep than Wakan and Acayla had ever seen. Dozens of herds were supervised by lone herders who sat near their round-topped wagons.

The sheep dogs also posed a danger. These animals were trained to fight wolves and chase coyotes from the area. They were aggressive, and while Wakan was not afraid of the dogs, he wanted to avoid any fights which might cause injury to his young family.

But as the troop traveled into unfamiliar territory, it was inevitable they would encounter the shepherds and their dogs.

One such incident came when they approached a large creek which flowed southward into the Moreau River.

There was a meadow filled with the woolly animals, all grazing quietly.

Wakan and his family had not eaten anything larger than rabbits for most of their trip and they were desperate for fresh meat.

The alpha wolf had always been cautious about attacking livestock inside the pastures, but these sheep in the open appeared to be fair game.

After the pack spotted the herd of sheep, the wolves withdrew to a hiding place near the creek to await darkness.

Acayla dictated the plan. They would move into the outer edges of the large herd after the sheep herder retired for the night.

Watching from a distance, the alpha female gave a signal to the members of the pack to maneuver themselves toward the herd.

Wakan and Acayla led the group consisting of Sapa, Ohake, Sapir and Topa.

The strategy was to remain out of sight of the dogs and the wagon.

The herd was settled down for the night when the wolves moved silently toward them. Without a sound, they slipped up on the docile animals and slashed their throats or broke their necks with ease.

Four ewes and six lambs lay dead in a matter of minutes.

The wolves ate their fill, surrounded by the rest of the sheep. While most of the animals milled around aimlessly, a few bleated in distress.

Wakan paid no attention. He knew they were too stupid to realize what had happened.

One older ewe took exception to the presence of the wolves, however, and began a constant "bah - bah - bah".

Wakan heard the sheep dogs barking. The disturbance woke the sheep herder. From the crest of a hill, Wakan watched the sheep herder light the lantern inside the wagon and emerge with a rifle in his hand.

The alpha wolf knew from experience that most sheep herders fired their guns in the air to scare the intruders away.

Believing that coyotes were attacking his flock, this man fired and then sent the dogs into the herd to chase away the interlopers. Wakan and his pack did not scare so easily.

Wakan and Acayla urged the others to abandon their meals and start back to the area where Laomi and the others waited.

They led Topa and Sapir away, but Ohake and Sapa remained to finish eating their fill.

Wakan ran back to warn them again just as the dogs raced toward the spot where the sheep carcasses were lying.

The herd scattered and left the shepherd an open view of the wolves in the moonlight.

He raised his rifle and shot. The first attempt missed, but he quickly shot again, this time wounding Ohake in the rear leg.

Yelping and crying in pain, Wakan's sister ran away from the danger with Sapa at her side.

The two wolves escaped the other bullets the man fired. The sisters ran toward Wakan. He escorted them away from the danger.

In a few moments the three caught up with Acayla and the two yearling pups. All six ran to the safety of the creek bottom.

Once away from the herd of sheep, the pack stopped long enough to look at Ohake's wound. The bullet had penetrated the skin and passed through the muscle just below the hip.

While the bullet tore the flesh, it did not break any bones. It was painful, but not fatal. Acayla helped Ohake lick the wound clean. The process of sanitizing the injury would help it heal.

Ohake was fortunate the bullet had not found a more vulnerable mark.

Sensing that the sheep herder had heard Ohake's screams when she was shot, Wakan felt the man might try to hunt down the wounded wolf. So for added safety, he ordered the family to leave the area within a couple hours of the shooting.

"Will you be able to travel?" Acayla inquired of Ohake.

"Yes," was the simple reply.

The family moved on; their way being lighted by the huge Hunter's Moon of October.

CHAPTER 18

Ohake's wound was severe enough to cripple her leg. She would be partially disabled for life.

After the initial escape from the herder and his dogs, the pack moved at a slow pace for several hours, allowing Ohake to keep up. They traveled in single file across the prairie, careful to remain out of sight of any homesteads, and watchful so as to not cross pastures where livestock were located.

Ohake often fell behind. She was forced to walk on three legs. Fatigue overcame her several times and she had to lie down to tend her wound.

"Wakan," Acayla motioned, "We must stop and let Ohake rest."

The alpha male agreed, "Now that we're far away from the man who shot her, we can look for a place to rest for a few days."

Wakan instructed Sapa to take Topa and Sapir to help her scout the area to find a suitable spot.

The female obeyed.

The three scouts headed south to look for a safe haven for the family.

As the search continued, they noticed there were fewer ranches and farms. Eventually the wolves crossed into the Cheyenne Indian Reservation.

Topa and Sapir continued to scent mark their trail as they progressed, hoping that Wakan and the others would be able to follow. Dawn was approaching when the trio reached the Moreau River. There they found an excellent sanctuary.

The trio had traveled all night; they were exhausted. Sapa motioned to the others to stay hidden and get some rest during the day.

The area was a secluded spot close to the water and well hidden from anyone who passed by. While Topa and Sapir found soft grass to lay in, Sapa napped briefly then began to explore the area. It was perfect. She was satisfied that this would be a safe place for the family.

Just before nightfall, Sapa left Topa and Sapir so as to return to lead the rest of the family to this spot.

"Don't stray away from this place," she instructed the yearling pups. "I will find everyone and return soon," she added.

She traveled more rapidly without the two younger wolves with her, covering nearly forty miles throughout the night. Early the next morning, she reached the area where she left Wakan, Acayla and the others. She was anxious to see Ohake and find out how her leg was healing.

She cautiously approached the small valley, sniffing the ground for signs of her family. When she couldn't locate them immediately, she feared that hunters had found the pack and driven them off.

Sapa searched for human scents or the smell of horses or dogs, but she found none.

Finally, after looking for several minutes, she picked up Wakan's familiar scent. He had left her a trail to follow.

The alpha male had moved his family to another valley a short distance away.

When she found them, Sapa joyfully greeted each member of the pack.

"Hunters have been in the area," Wakan indicated to Sapa. "We had to move, they were looking for us," he concluded.

"We have found a perfect place," Sapa communicated.

All the wolves gathered around as she tried to indicate where they were going to relocate.

"It will take us all night to get there," Sapa added. "Sapir and Topa are waiting for us there."

Acayla had a worried look, but Wakan went to her, offering reassurance, and indicating that they were old enough to take care of themselves.

"We should leave immediately," Acayla conveyed.

"We cannot go during daylight," Wakan responded.

Acayla agreed, "Yes, it is too dangerous." Yet she was anxious to check on the welfare of her two older pups.

Sapa went to the bed of grass where Ohake was resting. "Are you healing?" she inquired.

"Yes, but it's painful," her sister replied.

The family spent a restless day, trying to sleep, but anxious to be on their way south.

Near sunset, Wakan was unsettled. Finally he notified the family, "It's time to leave."

The wolves gathered around their alpha male and female for final instructions on the night's travel.

"Follow in a straight line," Wakan directed the pack.

"Keep Ohake between us," Acayla indicated to Sapa.

The pack left the hostile territory as the nighttime shadows filled the valley where they had taken refuge from their enemies.

They traveled several hours without interruption. Ohake kept pace with the others, indicating that her leg was not bothering her. She even mastered walking on three legs for most of the trip.

Shortly after midnight, Wakan found water in a small creek. The group rested there for about an hour before moving on.

By dawn, they had covered thirty miles.

"We can go on if you're strong enough," Wakan indicated to Ohake.

His sister responded that she was able to continue, so they proceeded, staying low in the valleys and gullies and avoiding any hilltops or mesas.

Sapa ran ahead of the group, searching for Sapir's and Topa's scent markings. She found them and directed the group toward the cottonwood trees along the shallow river in the distance.

Topa and Sapir, anxiously watching for their family to come, burst out of the washout where they were hiding the moment they saw the others approach.

Sapir had indicated to his brother that he picked up the scent of his father and mother long before they arrived. He had always displayed a keen sense of awareness of the location of prey and the whereabouts of family members.

The reunion was another joyous occasion, common to this family of wolves. Whenever they were separated, even for short periods of time, the brood always greeted one another with enthusiasm.

Wakan and Acayla fondled their two sons, giving them rewards for obeying Sapa's orders and staying hidden. The yearlings responded by jumping around, tails high in the air, begging to play tag.

Most of the family joined in the game of chasing each other around the meadow, biting at tails and hind legs and rolling in the tall soft grass.

Finally, tired of the romping, Wakan found a place to lie down to rest. The others took his hint and settled down for some well deserved relaxation.

Laomi, showing her age more than ever, managed to follow along on the arduous journey without complaining.

Now she took advantage of this peaceful place. As she lay resting, she remembered that she and Zando had once traveled close to the area where the Indians lived.

Her memory was fading somewhat, but she recalled that the Indians had not threatened them during that trip.

She hoped it would be the same for her family now.

After several hours rest, Wakan and Acayla led a hunting party of five, looking for prey. Within a few minutes, the group came across a herd of mule deer resting in the late afternoon sun.

The deer did not panic, but seemed curious about the wolves. It was apparent that they had not seen many wolves in their territory before.

"Stalk them carefully," Wakan warned. "We must be successful. It's been days since we ate anything larger than rabbits," he reminded the others.

Singling out a fat doe, the wolves surrounded the animal, allowing her no avenue of escape. She ran around in circles trying to elude the predators, but each time she tried to break through the wolves enclosure, they turned her away.

Finally, in confusion, the deer rushed directly toward Wakan. He leaped at her throat as she passed by him, his vice-like jaws grabbing her neck. Wakan's long, sharp fangs tore her hide. His hold on the doe's neck was unbroken in spite of her attempts to shake him off.

Within seconds, Acayla and Sapa assisted by dragging the deer down from behind, each of them hanging on her hind quarters.

The two younger wolves, Sapir and Topa joined in on the kill after the doe was on the ground. It was the first time their mother and father had taken them hunting and they were excited at the success they helped achieve.

There was enough meat for the whole pack. Sapir and Topa proudly returned to the sanctuary, their stomach's bloated with meat, anxious to disgorge their cargo for the others to consume.

Laomi and Ohake were the first to eat. Then the younger pups devoured the venison left by the adults.

Wakan watched over the carcass as the others returned to the meadow. He tore large pieces of flesh from the deer and stacked it up to be stored in a cache. He didn't want to leave the animal since he couldn't be sure a human would not place poison on the meat while the wolves were gone.

He saw to it that nothing was wasted. Soon, several of the other wolves returned to help carry the nourishment to a hiding place.

Life seemed tranquil for the pack during the next few weeks. Periodically, Wakan led exploration parties into the surrounding territory.

At times they saw Indian people riding in wagons and on horses, but they seldom saw any white men.

Nevertheless, he kept the pack away from all humans just to be on the safe side. He was watchful of all activity, but this was the longest period of time without attack by humans that he could remember.

Wakan possessed a strong intuition about different kinds of people. His remembrances and the knowledge passed on to him by Zando and Laomi, made to realize that he could trust the Indian people he encountered.

Meticulously he planned an experiment. He would get close to Indians to determine if they were hostile to wolves.

He didn't know which ones to approach, but felt he would be safer if he followed a wagon rather than a rider on horseback. He would have a much better chance of escaping from a team of horses pulling a wagon than from a rider.

Wakan decided to watch from a safe distance to determine if the Indians were armed. He had not seen any sign of rifles in earlier observations, but he wasn't going to take any chances.

Wakan also vowed to protect his family from all danger by giving them strict instructions to stay away from all humans, whether Indian or white man.

While the pack occupied themselves harvesting the abundant wild game in this area, Wakan began his escapade to study the Indians, attempting to determine if the positive relationship between these natives and wolves still existed.

CHAPTER 19

HAY - AY - AY - AY - AY - AY

Boom - boom - boom - boom. Boom - boom - boom - boom.

HAY - AY - AY - AY - AY - AY

Boom - boom - boom - boom. Boom - boom - boom - boom.

Wakan and Acayla stood quietly listening to the unusual sound echoing down the valley where they were scouting the new territory.

After listening for several minutes, the alpha pair crept slowly toward the sound.

HAY - AY - AY - AY - AY - AY.

Boom - boom - boom - boom. Boom - boom - boom - boom.

In the distance, Wakan and Acayla saw the figure of a man sitting on a rock outcrop at the top of a butte.

Cautiously they moved closer, careful not to expose themselves to dangers that might be nearby.

The uncommon sound continued.

HAY - AY - AY - AY - AY -AY.

Boom - boom - boom - boom. Boom - boom - boom - boom.

Wakan motioned to Acayla to creep up the side of the opposite hill, following the tall grass and sage brush in order to remain hidden.

When the source of the sound was plainly visible, they lay quietly in the tall grass watching. The sound came from an old Indian beating on a small hide-covered drum. They could see him rocking back and forth as he sang to the drumbeat.

HAY - AY - AY - AY - AY.

Boom - boom - boom - boom. Boom - boom - boom - boom..

Wakan and Acayla watched as the song continued for several minutes. Then suddenly it stopped.

The ancient Indian sat motionless.

They could see that he had set up a wickiup and built a small fire inside a circle of stones. Beside him was a colorful deer hide medicine bag lying open. The two wolves could see most of the contents of the bag, including a red stone pipe with a long, elaborately decorated stem, a half dozen arrows, a few small stones and a leather pouch.

The elderly Indian reached for the pipe and opened the small leather pouch. He stuffed a substance into the bowl of the pipe and picked up a small burning stick from the fire and placed it over the bowl.

Whiffs of smoke soon circled above the Indian's head as he puffed on the pipe.

The man stretched his arms out in front on him and raised the smoking pipe high in the air. Weaving from side to side, the Indian began another chant. This time in a softer voice and without the accompaniment of the drum.

IEEEE - EEE - EEE -EEE - EEE.

He repeated the refrain several times, puffing on the stem of the pipe between verses.

Wakan and Acayla watched intently. They had never seen an Indian during his prayer rituals. It was fascinating.

The Indian wore a headdress made of eagle feathers with a colorful beaded band across the forehead. His clothing was made from deer hide, elaborately painted with pictures of buffalo, a wolf and ravens.

Across from the Indian, at the entrance to the wickiup, was a bleached white buffalo skull. The man's attention focused on the skull as he continued to sing to and offer the smoking pipe to *nature's spirit*.

Patiently watching through the afternoon, Wakan and Acayla secretly moved away from their observation post and trotted back down the ravine toward the rendezvous site where the family waited.

Upon reaching the living area, Wakan transmitted the peculiar event to Laomi.

The elderly wolf listened intently, then indicated to her son that she wanted to see this phenomenon.

Wakan and Acayla agreed to lead her to the Indian after dark.

The sunset was spectacular. The thin rippling clouds reflected bright yellow close to the horizon, changing in layers to gold, orange, red and finally purple, high up in the western sky.

Wakan instructed the family to remain in the secure area while he, Acayla and Laomi were gone.

The three wolves moved out of the rendezvous area toward the site where the Indian was located.

When they arrived, Wakan could see by his silhouette that the man had not moved since their afternoon visit.

The Indian sat in front of the fire, head bowed as if napping.

Laomi, staring intently at the man, crept ahead of Wakan and Acayla to get a better view.

The old man raised his head and looked beyond the fire directly toward the spot where the three wolves lay hidden in the darkness.

The Indian then picked up the small drum and began a rhythmic beat.

BOOM - boom - boom

BOOM - boom - boom

BOOM - boom - boom.

He started his song. Quietly at first, then raising the volume as he continued.

HEY - YA

HEY - YA

HEY - YA.

His voice echoed down the valley and the still night air carried the sound across the prairie.

Laomi sat up on her haunches, looking intently at the Indian.

"What is it?" Wakan inquired.

Laomi was silent.

Wakan felt a strange sensation and shuddered.

"Something peculiar is happening," he signaled to Acayla.

The younger female continued to lay directly behind Laomi, observing the older wolf and watching the Indian chanting.

Laomi broke the silence, "We must move closer".

Wakan and Acayla followed the elder wolf down the hillside and part-way up the hill where the Indian was sitting.

When they had gotten to within a few yards, Laomi stopped and sat down.

Wakan and Acayla did the same, sitting slightly behind the old wolf.

Laomi continued her unblinking stare at the Indian.

"He is a medicine man," Laomi disclosed.

Wakan and Acayla did not respond.

"He is singing to the *nature's spirit* asking that the buffalo return to the prairie," she added.

Laomi listened to the man's voice, chanting in the darkness.

HI - EEE - AH

BOOM - boom - boom

HI - EEE - AH

BOOM - boom - boom

HI - EEE - AH.

"He's asking the *nature's spirit* to send the wolves to help the Indians find buffalo and hunt them," she proclaimed.

Laomi understood that the fulfillment of her life was near. She approached the elderly Indian, enchanted by his rhythmic song.

HI - EEE - AH

BOOM - boom - boom

Now she was only a few feet from the Shaman who continued beating his drum and chanting.

HI - EEE - AH.

BOOM - boom - boom.

Wakan and Acayla were witnessing a phenomenon. They had never seen a wolf come so close to a human.

Laomi sat down opposite the fire circle, never interrupting her fixed stare into the Indian's eyes. Her eyes reflected the yellow flames.

The Medicine Man's prayers were answered.

The Indian stopped singing. The drum beat ended. The silence was broken only by the crackling of the fire.

Then the Shaman began to speak, "Oh Great Spirit, you have answered the prayers of my people. We asked for the help of our friend the wolf, and you have sent her."

The ancient one continued, "Now we will find the buffalo which have hidden from us for so many moons. We will hunt the buffalo with our friends the wolves."

"This will give strength to my people, we will rule this land again and drive the white man away," he concluded.

Laomi stood transfixed.

Wakan and Acayla lay quietly in the shadows, staring at the events unfolding before them.

The wolves had no fear as all three concentrated on the thoughts of the Indian.

"Thank you, Great Spirit, for bringing this wolf to us," the Indian said.

Then he fell silent.

His thoughts lingered on the remembrances of his youth, before the white man invaded his land. A time when Indians roamed the prairies hunting buffalo and living in harmony with *nature's spirit*.

He recalled how the wolves and Indians respected the lives of their prey, how the meat of the animals they killed gave them strength and understanding of all living things.

"My people and you were companions and depended on each other for survival," he said, directing his words to Laomi.

"We must return to those times or we will all perish," he added, looking into her eyes.

Primeval thought messages were exchanged between the ancient Indian and the elderly wolf.

"We are brother and sister in nature," the Indian concluded.

Wakan looked intently at his mother.

She felt his stare and motioned to him to stay back.

"Do not approach," she admonished her son.

He obeyed.

"I must fulfill my purpose," she transmitted. "It is my duty to help my native brother," she resolved.

Laomi stood up as the Indian reached for a primitive bow lying at his side. Deliberately, he notched an arrow into the string. He pulled back the bow and let the arrow fly.

It passed through the leaping flames, directly into Laomi's heart. She slumped to the ground without a sound.

The Indian, tears streaming from his eyes, rose to his feet and approached Laomi.

AH - YEE - AHHH, he chanted, looking into the sky.

Sparks from the fire followed his prayer to the heavens.

Wakan and Acayla watched the rapid succession of events, but did not move.

Both were aware that Laomi had voluntarily sacrificed herself to the Medicine Man. They realized the ceremony was a necessary part of the Indian's prayer to the Great Spirit.

Neither became alarmed as the old Indian removed Laomi's skin and head with a few quick slashes of his old-fashioned flint knife.

When the operation was completed, he removed his headdress and placed Laomi's skull on top of his head with the hide hanging loosely down his back.

Then, with his tired legs aching, the old man began dancing in a circle around the ceremonial fire. With slow and unsteady steps, he held Laomi's hide around him, her white coat glistening in the darkness.

The Shaman sang the ancient song of thanksgiving to the Great Spirit, asking that the *spirit of nature* return to his people.

The ceremony continued for hours. The old man chanted until his voice broke from strain. Then, exhausted, the Indian lay down next to the dying embers of the fire.

Wakan and his mate were motionless, absorbing every action.

Finally at dawn, the pair approached the sleeping Indian, sniffed the skin of the wolf they both loved so dearly, and bid Laomi farewell.

The companions left the scene deeply moved. They had witnessed a ritual dating back to prehistoric times. They understood, but they could not perceive that this attempt by the spiritual leader of the Plains Indians was to restore what could never exist again.

But there was no sadness for Wakan and Acayla. They knew that Laomi had fulfilled her destiny and had passed to the animal's *spirit world*.

CHAPTER 20

The warm spring weather was a welcome relief from the long Dakota winter.

Wakan and Acayla took every opportunity to enjoy their family and spent hours playing with each member. The snow was nearly melted except for the deep drifts which were hidden from the gentle sunshine.

The family had survived another year and the refreshing weather brought them all back together in preparation for Acayla's impending delivery of a new batch of pups.

The birth of the pups was still a few weeks away and Wakan and Acayla took advantage of the beautiful spring weather while looking for a whelping den.

The alpha pair were playfully running through a clearing where fresh new grass was sprouting. Early spring prairie flowers were already in bloom, peeking through the dried brown grass left from last season.

Wakan always enjoyed Acayla's companionship.

As they were ducking around the trees along a dry creek bed, the pair stopped periodically to exchange affectionate nuzzles and bites around the face and neck.

Acayla rolled on to her back in front of her mate, pawing at him as he approached.

Wakan mouthed her throat with an affectionate growl and stepped over her reclining body. As he stood over her, he noticed her mammary's were beginning to enlarge in preparation for feeding the new puppies.

Acayla stood upright, diving at Wakan's tail and capturing it in her mouth.

Wakan responded by biting on to her tail and the pair moved in circles until both lost their balance and fell over.

Acayla then started to run away from her mate, looking back to see how close he was to catching her.

As the two wolves reached the wooded edge of the clearing, shots rang out.

Instantly Acayla's body slammed into a large ash tree a few feet ahead of Wakan.

His immediate reaction was to rush to her but his instincts caused him to lie flat on the ground, motionless.

From where he lay hidden, Wakan could see the unmoving body of his mate ten yards ahead.

A feeling of fear ran through him. A terror that he had never known before.

He felt a driving urge to go to Acayla's side, yet he knew the riflemen were nearby. He needed to see if he could help Acayla get up and run away from the danger.

Still, he realized that because she did not move, she must be mortally wounded.

Slowly Wakan crawled toward Acayla. He could see a slight heave of her sides as he got closer. He didn't dare take a chance of raising up to look for the hunters. He would have to gamble that they could not see him crawling through the grass.

When he reached his mate's side he nudged her with his muzzle. She did not move. Slowly Wakan raised his paw, placing it on her neck, shaking her slightly.

After a long moment, Acayla raised her head, her eyes were only slightly open. As she turned her head, Wakan could see a gaping wound in her neck and shoulder. He realized the bullet wound was fatal and that she would bleed to death in a few moments.

Wakan pushed his nose under her chin. She rested her head on it. Then she raised her head and licked Wakan's muzzle. He responded.

Then the beautiful Acayla's head fell to the ground with one final moan.

She was gone.

Wakan was stunned.

As he lay beside her body, he felt the movement of the tiny bodies inside her. Wakan realized that their children would die with her and he was powerless to do anything about it.

For the first time in his life he did not know what to do. He lay motionless next to her body.

The emotional scene lasted only a minute. Wakan heard the riflemen on their horses, riding through the nearby brush.

Wakan wanted to stay by his loving mate's side, not caring whether the hunters found him. He had never known such a loss. Even when Zando was shot, or when his mother died, he did not experience the dread he now felt.

As the voices of the riders reached him, his instincts took over. He knew he must leave Acayla and lead the hunters away from the rest of the family.

He licked Acayla's lifeless lips one more time, then quietly crawled into the deep grass.

Wakan knew that there had been two shots. The one aimed at him missed, hitting the ground a few yards beyond him.

That meant that the hunters knew he was there and would be looking for him. Wakan's experience with hunters told him that they would expect him to run away from them.

Instead, he crouched low and crawled at an angle toward the hunters, moving in time with the motion of the grass waving in the wind.

Years of evading ranchers, trappers and hunters, taught Wakan to do the unexpected.

He continued to crawl until he reached the small dry creek. Before easing down into the creek bed, he listened for the men's voices. He could hear them clearly as they moved toward Acayla's body.

"I know I got one of them," a voice proclaimed.

"Yea, but where is it?" another asked.

"Keep your eyes peeled for that gray," a third ordered.

They were heading straight for Acayla.

Wakan waited until they passed. He lay flat on the ground. They did not see him. They were too busy looking for his mate's body and scanning the area beyond where Acayla lay. It was obvious his ploy was working since they were not looking to either side.

When the riders moved on, Wakan eased down into the creek bed. He would have to be careful not to be caught in this enclosure since he would have little cover in which to hide.

Periodically, he peeked over the side of the embankment to see if the hunters had caught on to his maneuver. So far he was lucky.

His immediate priority was to escape, to somehow lead the shooters away from the pack.

Wakan knew when the men found Acayla's body, they would see his tracks and identify "Three Toes."

He was right.

He was far enough away from the riders now so that he could not hear their words. There was a lot of excitement and shouting.

Once he was certain he was beyond the range of their rifles, Wakan climbed out of the creek on the opposite bank. Loping to a small rise, he looked toward the spot where Acayla was shot.

He stood in full view of the hunters, quietly watching for several minutes, until one of them looked up and saw him.

"There he is," he shouted.

Another raised his rifle and shot. The bullet hit the ground several yards short of its mark.

Wakan turned and started running in the opposite direction from where his family was located.

One of the riders placed a rope on Acayla's body as the other two mounted their horses and started riding toward Wakan.

Now Wakan's goal was to put as much distance as possible between himself and the hunters. If they continued to track him, the pack would be safe.

He headed for the area just below a line of high rocky hills. He could move through this rugged area much faster than the horses and he knew dozens of small caves where he could hide from his pursuers.

Every few minutes, the elusive wolf stopped, turned sideways in full view of the riders, and stood watching them.

Whenever he did this, the hunters could not ignore the urge to shoot at him, even though he was dozens of yards out of rifle range.

Wakan's plan was to continue leading the hunters away from his pack, high into the desolate hills where they would not be able to see his tracks. Then he would disappear from sight.

He knew his pursuers well enough to know that they would continue to look for him for an hour or so, then give up the chase.

After a few more episodes of standing in full view watching the men pursue him, Wakan faded into the landscape. They had no idea where he went.

High up in the buttes, Wakan found a small depression among the rocks. His gray coat blended perfectly with the background. There, he lay watching his pursuers.

Anger boiled inside him as he watched the third hunter approach the two who were chasing him. The man was abusing Acayla's body by dragging it behind his horse.

Strong urges rose up deep in his stomach. He started to get up out of his hiding spot. His heart ached for his beloved mate, but he knew he could not attack the hunters successfully.

It bothered Wakan that he could have been so careless. Both he and Acayla had missed sensing the presence of the hunters.

Now the unthinkable tragedy had struck. Acayla was dead.

One moment of carelessness had cost her life and nearly his own. The more he thought about it, the more enraged he became.

Wakan wanted to rush down the hillside and attack the riders, knock them down from their horses and rip open their throats, but he knew he would have no chance against the rifles and the fast horses.

He would have to vent his wrath another way. This treachery could not pass without retaliation.

Wakan vowed that he would even the score, though he realized nothing would bring back his cherished Acayla.

CHAPTER 21

After the riders departed, Wakan lay on the hillside for several hours. He watched the hunters ride away, jubilant over their kill.

When the sun began to set, he emerged from his hiding place.

Wakan had stayed there, not so much to avoid meeting the ranchers again, but to give the tragedy of Acayla's death time to penetrate his mind.

He made his way back to the area where the pack was waiting for their alpha male and female to return.   This catastrophe would shock the family.

Wakan and Acayla made a special effort to be sure that all members of the pack felt important. Each individual knew they were loved and esteemed. The two leaders were very successful in keeping the family close. This was a great advantage since each wolf knew his role in the scheme of things and was respected for what they contributed.

Now, with Acayla gone, Wakan's leadership role would change.

He would no longer have the support and wisdom of his mate. He would have to deal with restructuring the pack and intensify his training of a successor.

This episode was a reminder that he could fall victim to the humans at any time. If the pack was to survive, he must make preparations.

As he made his way back, Wakan's thoughts turned to the present. How would he break the news to his children and the rest of the pack?

Many other thoughts crowded Wakan's mind, but he decided to set them aside until the family finished mourning Acayla's death.

Darkness had fallen by the time Wakan arrived at the rendezvous site. The pack had expected their leaders to return hours ago.

Every wolf rushed toward Wakan as he approached. His sister Sapa was the first to reach him.

"Where's Acayla," she inquired.

Wakan did not answer.

The others gathered around him, curious as to whether he and Acayla had made a kill. They nipped at his mouth in an effort to get him to regurgitate. He ignored their efforts.

Finally, after it was apparent that Wakan was not going to respond to any of their communications, the pack settled down.

Wakan stood silently for a long moment. The young wolves, unaware of the drama of the moment, tried to get Sapa and Ohake to play with them.

Both of Wakan's sisters knew him well enough to understand something was wrong.

"Where's Acayla?" Sapa insisted.

"Dead," was the reply.

The rendezvous site became silent.

Ignoring the traditional rule not to stare into the eyes of the alpha male, every member of the family looked directly at Wakan.

There would be no further explanation.

There was no need.

After a few moments, each wolf turned and walked to a secluded spot to lie down.

The family remained silent for several hours. Finally, as the nearly full moon rose over the Slim Buttes, Wakan stood up and trotted to a hilltop.

There he began a slow, mournful howl. The sound began deep in his chest and erupted through his throat and hollow mouth.

For several minutes, Wakan stood alone, continuing the pain filled sounds.

After a time, Sapa rose from her resting place and stood beside her brother. She too released a long, chilling howl into the night air.

Then Ohake joined her siblings, then Sapir and Topa, Newah, and Caldra.

Ajule, Laka, Broz and Tam, the youngest pups, not yet a year old, merged their immature voices with the rest.

This night would linger in the pack's memories forever. Only Wakan, Ohake and Sapa remembered the pain the family suffered when Zando died.

While the whole family was saddened when Laomi died the winter before, the impact of her death was much different.

They had never witnessed anything so somber as this night.

After nearly an hour of constant howling, it suddenly stopped. No signal was given, but everyone knew that this phase of the mourning process was over.

Wakan led the pack back down the hill to the rendezvous site.

The younger members found their favorite sleeping place and curled up under Ohake's supervision.

Sapa stood next to her brother, comforting him as best she could. In a few moments, Sapir joined his father and aunt. The three stood in a circle, each with their heads on the others backs. Touching was the only communication necessary.

Finally, Wakan moved away from the others and sat down near a clearing in the trees. He sat, staring out into the silent darkness. Sapa and Sapir found their beds and went to sleep.

The shock began wear off. Schemes generated in Wakan's mind as he sat contemplating what changes he would make.

Again, he thought of the pack and how it must survive. Sapa was a strong leader and she would be a great help.

Sapir was now three years old and ready to take on more responsibilities.

He had already functioned as the beta male and knew how to track and stalk game, but he needed additional instruction on how to deal with humans.

Because Ohake was crippled, her capacity to lead was limited. She would have to replace Acayla in caring for the four youngest pups.

Topa, Newah, and Caldra would be helpful in capturing prey. Each had learned their lessons well.

The pack would survive but there was much to do.

The moment Wakan stopped thinking about the responsibilities of the family members, the simmering anger began to swell inside him.

He had difficulty not yielding to hatred. He realized that if he dwelled on his malice toward the men who shot Acayla, he would not be able to concentrate on his family responsibilities.

During the weeks that followed Acayla's death, Wakan focused on making things as normal as possible for the pack.

He assigned Sapa the responsibilities for hunting. She had Laomi's instincts for detecting game and had become proficient at stalking and attacking. Wakan also saw to it that Topa, Newah and Caldra accompanied Sapa on the hunting expeditions.

Wakan delegated Ohake to care for the pups full time. The others would be responsible for bringing food for them until the pups were old enough to accompany the adults on hunting parties.

Sapir received Wakan's full attention.

The alpha wolf spent hours honing his son's instincts, teaching him responsibilities of leadership, instructing him in the art of commanding respect, and tutoring him in the knowledge of their worst enemy, man.

Wakan found that the final area of Sapir's education was most difficult. This was the task of enlightening him in the understanding of the wolf's role in the wild and wolves' relationship with *nature's spirit*.

Wakan knew that Sapir would have a hard time understanding this because the wolf's environment had changed so dramatically in the past two generations.

Wakan remembered the lessons Zando had passed on to him as he was maturing. Wakan understood much of what his father was relaying to him, but even his generation lived entirely different than did his father, grandfather and great-grandfather.

Since the Indian left the plains and the white man devoured the wolf's territory, the instincts of the past no longer applied.

It would take a new wisdom to survive. Wakan was frustrated because he felt inadequate to pass this discernment on to his offspring.

For thousands of years, wolves lived on what nature provided. They lived in harmony with Indians, each assuming responsibility for their purpose in life.

Three generations before Wakan was born, the white man began his invasion.

First the mountain men came. But their damage was small, they were few in numbers and generally stayed out of the wolf's locale.

Next came the soldiers. There were more of them and they inflicted immeasurable harm on the wolf's environment by destroying millions of buffalo. The soldiers also killed the native people and took the survivors away from their lands.

The Indians, who were compatible with wolves, were replaced by the white men who came to this territory with their unreasonable fear and hatred for wolves.

Wakan spent hours in an effort to impress this upon Sapir. Some of what he communicated was historical knowledge of how things used to be, and some was wishful thinking about how he would like things to be again.

Sapir listened intently. He absorbed as much information as he could understand, but much of the traditional consciousness escaped him.

Wakan recognized this and understood that things had changed so dramatically in recent years that Sapir probably would not find this knowledge useful.

The alpha wolf decided he should concentrate on those things which would help Sapir keep himself and their family alive.

"We must observe how man functions," Wakan transmitted to Sapir.

"We will follow them to examine their habits and learn more about how we can avoid their traps and poisons," he added.

Sapir accompanied his father on several trips, watching how the humans handled their livestock and what they did when they placed traps or poison settings.

Experience had taught Wakan how to detect even the slightest scent of humans, their steel traps, and poison.

After they observed one man setting a baited trap, he took Sapir to the area to familiarize him with the smells and surroundings.

Meanwhile, Sapa kept a tight rein on the activities of the pack. She had been fairly successful in hunting game and bringing home enough food to sustain the family.

Sapa continued to teach the younger wolves, and all of them showed signs of becoming excellent hunters.

She also disciplined each one with regard to their going anywhere near carcasses which most wolves found tempting. The remembrance of Nehma and Ozhe's deaths were still strongly implanted in her mind, and she did everything she could to keep that incident from being repeated.

Ohake excelled at teaching the youngest wolves. She showed patience and understanding and helped them understand their future role within the pack.

The youngsters were becoming self-sufficient in catching small game and were excellent stalkers.

Wakan was pleased with the progress shown by everyone. He continued to concentrate on Sapir and felt the wolf was nearly ready to assume leadership.

"We all exist to serve the others in our family," he admonished.

"Each of you is important, each of you has a function which cannot be performed by anyone else," he continued.

"In the past weeks, you have all learned what you are best at. Some are good at tracking, some have great speed, some have excellent instincts for detecting prey or danger," Wakan instructed.

"Remain loyal to your family and serve one another. If you do that, you will overcome all adversity," he concluded.

Wakan felt a sense of relief that his family was prepared for the future.

Now, he would allow himself to indulge in his obsession, that of gaining revenge on those who slaughtered his Acayla.

CHAPTER 22

During the seven years of his life, Wakan witnessed fourteen members of his family die violently at the hands of humans.

Throughout his young adulthood he tried to suppress a growing anger over the way humans treated his species.

Even after his father was killed, he attempted to establish a positive relationship with humans.

He recalled the time he led the rancher to safety during a blizzard and other instances when he approached humans, curious about their ways.

After Zando was killed, Wakan saw his mother become deeply depressed. It affected both he and Sapa. The joy of being reunited with Acayla, Ohake and Nehma set the despair aside for a few months, but then it grew again as the attacks by ranchers continued.

As the years passed, he became embittered toward man. Bitterness was then replaced by hatred when his son Ozhe and brother Nehma ate poison. And finally after the sadness of Acayla's death, hatred was replaced by a desire for revenge.

Wakan's malice toward humans continued to grow, but he also realized that if he retaliated against man for what he had done to his family, he would bring even more reprisals against wolves.

Spending much of his time meditating on what to do, Wakan finally decided on a way to get even with the humans, yet avoid repercussions.

His plan demanded dramatic action.

Wakan knew he must lead his pack away from this area and re-establish them in a less populated territory. This would provide relative safety for his family, and he would be free to return to take revenge against the people who killed his loved ones.

The summer had nearly ended when Wakan gathered his family together. He communicated his plan to lead them out of the region to a safe place. He did not elaborate on the other part of his scheme, concerned that there might be some argument about his leaving the pack.

That night, the entire family of eleven wolves made their way single file out of the Slim Buttes toward the Montana border.

They traveled mainly by night, hunting when necessary, and resting during the day near the carcass of the animal they had slain the night before.

Wakan led the group west until they reached the Little Missouri River. They turned north, following the river until it wound its way east.

The wolves then headed northwest toward the Yellowstone River and followed it until they reached the Missouri.

The pack arrived at the muddy Missouri River just before sunrise eight days after they left their home territory. Wakan ordered the family to rest while he, Sapa, Newah, Topa, and Sapir went to search for game.

Wakan instructed Caldra to stay with Ohake and the pups. Ohake's crippled leg gave her a great deal of difficulty and she often fell behind the rest of the pack during the long trip.

She continued to watch over the youngsters, but they were so active and full of energy that she could no longer keep up with them.

Deer were abundant where Wakan led his little hunting party. About a hour before sunrise, they discovered a large herd which had just settled down after spending the night grazing.

They pursued two of the older deer about four miles before one of them finally decided to turn and fight. That was a fatal mistake.

Wakan and Sapa circled around behind while Sapir and Topa faced the deer straight on. Newah angled in from the side and when the deer turned to avoid the attack, all five converged on him.

There was very little struggle and the event was over in a few minutes.

Famished from their exhausting travels, the wolves devoured most of the prime flesh of the animal in less than an hour.

Immediately, all five, with their stomachs filled to capacity, left the deer carcass and returned to the other pack members.

They disgorged a portion of the venison for everyone who had been left behind. Their appetites satisfied, the whole family settled down for a day-long rest before attempting to cross the river.

Late in the afternoon, Wakan alerted the family that it was time to make the crossing. He wanted to get across the river while it was still daylight in case any of the members had difficulty.

"You lead the pack," Wakan instructed Sapa.

"I will swim across last to make sure the youngsters make it," he added.

The wolves entered the water reluctantly. They could tell there was a strong flow and many swirling undercurrents. Cautiously, they left the sandy bank and began swimming.

The strength of the current surprised them all. They had crossed many rivers in their lifetime, but never one which flowed with such force.

Paddling with all their strength, the river carried the wolves downstream. The uneven current separated them, and Wakan was concerned that some members might be lost.

Just as that thought crossed his mind, he saw Ohake struggling to keep her head above water.

Wolves are excellent swimmers and paddle strongly with their front legs.

Ohake, however, was suffering cramps in her crippled rear leg and could not maintain the strong effort it took to get across.

Wakan, paddling with just his head above the water, watched helplessly as Ohake went under the surface. The alpha male continued to search the river for her to resurface, but she did not.

When he reached the opposite shore, Sapa greeted him. She had also witnessed Ohake's disappearance.

Confident that she would drift safely to the shore further downstream, the two moved in that direction. Along the way, the rest of the family came ashore, coughing and spitting the muddy river water from their mouths, and shaking their drenched coats.

Sapa took inventory of the family.

"Everyone's here except Ohake," she indicated.

Wakan signaled to Sapa and the others to wait where they were. He began to search the river banks downstream.

An hour later he returned.

"I did not find her," he indicated.

"She did not come to shore on this side, and I don't think she had strength enough to swim back to the other bank," he concluded.

Sadly, the wolf pack left the river and began their night-long journey northward.

Two days later they arrived in the Moose Mountain area of Saskatchewan, Canada.

Wakan ordered the pack to investigate the territory.

It was obvious that several wolf packs inhabited the territories they crossed, and here they would have to carve out their own niche or find a neutral area which was undisputed.

After exploring and smelling the scent markings left by the existing packs, Wakan concluded that there was a fairly large area nearby which was uninhabited.

In the next few weeks, there were several minor skirmishes with established wolf packs who resented the intruders. However, Wakan and his clan managed to avoid any serious fights and found relative peace in the broad Canadian countryside.

The autumn season was much shorter in this new territory than the pack was accustomed to. Snow began to fall in September. By October it was obvious they would have to contend with the white stuff for several months.

There was excellent hunting, and Sapir, Sapa and Newah soon discovered moose. This animal brought a whole new hunting experience to the family.

Sapir had welcomed a four-year-old lone female into the pack shortly after they arrived. The wolf had apparently been expelled from a nearby pack by the alpha female. This often happened when the alpha female felt threatened by another female in the pack.

Wakan recognized that Sapir would mate with this northern wolf. She would help them adjust to the new territory and teach them methods of hunting moose and other prey unfamiliar to his pack.

Wakan was satisfied his family was safely relocated in an area where humans were seldom seen and where prey was abundant.

The harsh Dakota winters had prepared the pack for the difficult weather, and he knew they could survive without complications.

Wakan was ready to return to his native territory. The day he chose to leave, the weather was calm and warm. Very little snow had accumulated and the sky was clear.

Wakan gathered his entire pack together.

Sapir and the other wolves were standing in the center of a grove of trees watching their leader.

Wakan approached Sapir, but before the young male could lower his head in deference to the alpha, Wakan did something totally unexpected.

He lowered his body and slowly crawled up to Sapir, whining and pulling his lips back in a friendly smile. His tail was lowered and he turned his head to the side, completely submitting to Sapir's authority.

Sapir was totally shocked. He did not know what to do. His father had been a strong uncompromising leader all his adult life. The young male could not understand what was happening.

Sapa stood nearby, astounded. Ever since she and Wakan were puppies, he had always been dominant. She wondered how he could possibly submit to any other wolf. She had never seen him defer to anyone except Acayla, whom he always considered his equal.

Every wolf in the pack was watching intently. Even the yearlings stopped their playful frolicking to witness this historic event.

No member of the pack had ever witnessed an alpha male relinquish his role. This usually happened only when the leader was killed or became too old or weak to continue his responsibilities.

Wakan was none of these. He was a strong virile male in his prime. But tonight the leadership was changing voluntarily. Everyone knew something important was happening. They could not believe it.

When Wakan reached Sapir, he rolled over on his back just beneath Sapir's neck. He licked the young wolf's neck and lower jaw.

Sapir stood stiff legged. He received the message clearly, but was reluctant to accept it.

Wakan did not prolong the ceremony. He stood up, tail lowered, and moved quickly away from Sapir. He stopped momentarily at each member of the pack, nuzzling them on the face and neck and touching the heads of the youngsters.

Finally he came to Sapa. Wakan motioned to her and the two trotted away from the remainder of the family.

"You need to stay with Sapir and his new mate," he indicated.

"I want to go with you," she replied.

"They will need your help and you must stay," he admonished.

"But where are you going?" she questioned.

"Back to our home territory," he responded.

"I must do something that is too dangerous for any of you to be involved in," he concluded.

Licking his sister's mouth and face, Wakan said goodby.

The farewell's concluded, Wakan moved into the bright moonlight and started trotting away from the pack.

Instinctively, many started to follow. He turned and growled fiercely, warning them to stay back.

Sapir stood still. The full realization of what had occurred was just now soaking in.

For a few moments he watched Wakan as he continued to turn on members of the family, forcing them back.

Then Wakan stopped and looked directly at Sapir. He stared intently, sending a message that it was time for his son to take over leadership.

Sapir watched the flashing glow of Wakan's eyes. This was a look Sapir feared and respected.

That night, however, Sapir was not afraid. He knew that Wakan was transmitting, "Become their leader."

Sapir broke the silence with a shrill howl.

All eyes turned to him.

He howled again.

The message commanded the pack to follow him.

While the family gathered behind Sapir, Wakan disappeared into the darkness, away from his family, and toward an uncertain destiny.

CHAPTER 23

Wakan began his life as a "loner". Never again would he associate with any other wolf pack.

He made the trip from Canada in five days, travelling nearly non stop back to the home he loved.

While his family still lived with him, Wakan's motives were centered on the survival of the pack. This had been the way of wolves for centuries. His ancestors had lived out the role designed for them by nature.

Wakan had those instincts. He knew the way things should be. But man had changed the natural structure of life for this animal.

For centuries wolves occupied the entire continent. The land was virtually untouched by humans.

Then a different kind of man came and changed everything.

Great herds of elk which roamed the prairie were hunted nearly to extinction. Surviving herds were driven back into the high mountains of the west.

Herds of deer and pronghorn diminished through the wasteful hunting practices of man.

Even the immense flocks of geese and ducks were now just a memory as the result of the wholesale slaughter by humans.

The enormous herds of bison, the basic food supply for both wolves and Indians, were methodically wiped out by these newcomers.

Wakan's instinctive remembrances caused him to understand the special relationship wolves had with all wildlife. Deep inside him was the desire to perpetuate that link. But changes he could not control destined him to become one of the last wolves to live in this part of the world.

Zando had relayed to Wakan his memories of his father's and grandfather's packs and how changes had taken place. But those changes were slow. Only a limited number of humans came into their territory during those years following the soldiers occupation and the removal of the plains Indians.

Wakan knew the difficulty his father experienced trying to maintain a normal life style.

As the number of cattle and sheep ranches increased, so did the number of hunters and trappers who came to protect the domestic herds.

By the time Wakan took over the pack, circumstances had changed so dramatically that there was little for his family to do but battle against stupendous odds just to survive from day to day.

When he made his decision to move his family away from the territory, he was doing so in order to help them regain some semblance of "normal" life. He wanted his children and grandchildren to live as his father and the generations before them had lived.

In the first few days after leaving his family, Wakan experienced sadness. But he knew he had done what was best. Now his only emotion was anger.

Wakan's anger continued to grow as his thoughts turned to Acayla, his father, and to all the other loved ones he lost to the white man's hatred and superstition.

From the time he left his family in the relative safety of the north country, Wakan thought of little else but revenge. Hatred built up in him, a hatred toward man and all he owned.

On the night he arrived back in his territory, Wakan began a rampage which would make him notorious.

Winter came about the time Wakan arrived. The blustery wind foretold an early winter. Snow was falling steadily as he skirted a new sheep pasture built in the center of his territory.

Wakan left a greeting message by killing ten head of yearlings, eating only the liver of one of the animals.

The second night he moved to an adjacent area and killed a two-year-old steer, breaking the animal's neck with his powerful jaws.

Night after night, Wakan moved from pasture to pasture, randomly killing dozens of domestic animals.

Wakan's movements were not without strategy. He was constantly on the alert for ranchers or hunters in the area, and he observed every unusual landmark as a potential danger.

In retaliation, the ranchers set more traps and increased the number of poison sets. But Wakan detected every effort they made to capture him.

Wakan spent the entire winter in an area fifty miles wide and a hundred miles long, moving between ranches and herds grazing on the open prairie.

The number of calves, sheep and colts he killed that winter numbered in the hundreds.

Frustrated at being outwitted by this wolf, the ranchers hired professional trappers to track him down.

Wakan entered into what was to become one of the most fierce rivalries ever recorded between man and wolf.

The entire region spoke the name they had given this unique animal. Everyone knew about "Three Toes".

Wakan was blamed for nearly every animal death that took place in the territory.

Often when coyotes killed young sheep or calves, "Three Toes" was blamed even though he was never near the scene.

He continued to be a mystery to those who hunted him because of his ability to outmaneuver those pursuing him.

He instinctively planned every action, hunting by night and keeping himself well hidden when he slept during the day. He became a master at backtracking and traveling in rocky areas where it was impossible for hunting dogs to track him.

In the second year of his killing rampage three riders came upon a scene where Wakan had slaughtered two dozen sheep and had left his tracks plainly visible.

These hunters were hired by the local ranchers to track down their enemy.

Wakan watched the riflemen as they inspected the carnage he had left. When they found a clear set of tracks and began to ride toward him, Wakan loped to the crest of a hill, watching the men.

One of them spotted the wolf and shouted his discovery. All three urged their horses toward the sole object of their pursuit.

Wakan started across the prairie, keeping well ahead of the trio, but showing himself periodically. He kept up this pace throughout the day.

Toward evening, Wakan passed within a mile of a ranch house. With the light fading, the riders decided to stop for the night and take up the chase the next morning.

Wakan found a secure resting place near the top of a nearby butte where he could observe everything that occurred below.

Darkness and hunger settled in on Wakan simultaneously.

He saw a herd of sheep in a small pasture located next to the horse corral. Stealthily he moved down the hillside toward the animals.

Entering the distant end of the pasture, he moved toward the docile critters. Without remorse, he killed every one of the fifteen lambs in the pen. After eating portions of only one, Wakan systematically dragged each lamb to a gate post next to the corral and placed them in a pile.

Wakan then returned to his observation post high on the hill and napped throughout the night.

The next morning the riders could not avoid seeing his handiwork as they saddled their horses to continue to stalk him.

As the sun rose, the wolf was alert to the movement around the cabin and corral. He heard one of the men shout obscenities when he discovered the slain lambs.

Obviously angry, the three riders quickly saddled their horses, swung the rancher's gate open wide, and started to search for the tracks leading away from the dead animals.

"It's Three Toes," one shouted.

"The bastard came in here last night and killed these sheep right under our noses," another declared.

Wakan could sense their exasperation and outrage as he watched them locate his trail and begin to follow.

Minutes later, Wakan stood up from his bed of grass and loped over the hill in plain view of the riders. They rode past the matted-down bed where he slept, pointing to the spot and commenting on how close the wolf had been to them as they slept the night before.

The chase began for a second day. Wakan maintained a steady pace, just out of rifle range, but close enough to give his pursuers hope that they could catch him.

About mid-day, Wakan scared up a jackrabbit. After a short chase, the wolf caught the unfortunate animal and devoured it. The riders found the rabbit's remains as they passed, still doggedly following his distinct trail.

When night came, the riders were still tracking Wakan but could not catch up to him. That day their pursuit changed direction. After leading them north for a day and a half, "Three Toes" was now heading east.

During the night, while the hunters were explaining their disappointments to the rancher who lived nearby, Wakan found several cows and calves in a pasture about a mile from the ranch house.

He moved into the enclosure and attacked three of the calves, killing them instantly. Eating his fill, the wolf then walked back to within a few hundred yards of the house and watched as the humans doused their light and settled down to sleep for the night.

When morning arrived, Wakan was ready to lead them on the third and final leg of their fruitless journey.

All through the day, the riders followed the tireless wolf. They exchanged their exhausted horses that morning at a nearby ranch. They were confident they could outdistance "Three Toes".

Wakan sensed the riders were pursuing him at a faster pace so he increased his own stride, occasionally running rather than trotting, but always staying well ahead of his trackers.

A few hours later, Wakan turned his path southward, keeping a steady gait and periodically showing himself to the riders.

Late that afternoon, Wakan led the riders to within a mile of the ranch where the chase had begun three days before.

Wakan had escorted these hunters on a one hundred fifty mile wild goose chase.

He permitted them one last glance at him as he crossed over a hill in the distance. Then he disappeared from sight.

That night, Wakan rested before starting his journey east, moving out of the territory where he was pursued so relentlessly.

None of the rancher's or their hired hunters could guess where "Three Toes" would turn up next. He wandered over a large area, successfully carrying out his intention to destroy as many of the ranchers animals as possible.

In the months that followed, Wakan avoided every attempt to trap him. Occasionally he would pick up a small dead tree branch with his mouth, carry it to a suspected trap site, and spring the device with the wood.

Other times he would scratch dirt and debris onto a trap, causing it to spring shut from the added weight.

Wakan's sense of smell improved as he grew older. He could detect the scent of human activity around every trap or poison setting. Often he urinated on strychnine laced carcasses, leaving his tell-tale tracks beside the baited animal.

Wakan found several animals trapped in the settings meant for him. Sometimes other wolves that were passing through the area would fall victim to the steel monsters.

Hunters and trappers often found "Three Toes'" tracks next to their quarry, as if he had paid them his last respects before moving on.

And still, Wakan continued to inflict his vengeance on those who had destroyed much of his family.

Ranchers counted thousands of dead of cattle, sheep and horses, and laid the blame on "Three Toes".

They placed a bounty on him and offered rewards for those who could put a stop to his wanton destruction of livestock.

Often during his travels, Wakan's curiosity about man overcame his timidity toward them.

He followed individual riders and men driving teams of horses pulling wagons. During such visits he displayed caution, but seemed to sense the people he followed were not armed and would do him no harm.

The human world spread the news of this renegade wolf, but Wakan could not be aware of his notoriety.

Both believed the other perpetuated the cycle of animosity between them. The more attempts man made on "Three Toes'" life, the more animals he slaughtered in retaliation.

Man did not calculate the impact the wanton slaughter of Wakan's family would have on this wolf.

Man did not foresee that a wolf would have the ability to strike back.

Man lacked an understanding of Wakan's ability to execute plans of mass destruction of livestock and his competence in avoiding capture.

What man imagined to be viciousness, was simply reprisal for their own transgressions against Wakan's family.

CHAPTER 24

Driven by hatred for those who conducted the relentless massacre of his family, Wakan continued his rampage.

Alone now, the wolf established a pattern which would allow him to elude the pursuing hunters. He moved rapidly between ranches, killing sheep, cattle and occasionally, horses. He struck with swift and deadly accuracy.

Wakan satisfied his appetite with deer and other wild game he killed. But he was driven to slaughter as many of mans domestic livestock as he could, even though he seldom ate any portion of his kill.

It had been three years since Acayla's death. Wakan thought of her often, reflecting back on the times when he and his family lived together.

Wakan randomly attacked the livestock on every ranch in his path, but he selected two where he vented his particular hatred.

One was a large ranch where Zando and the other members of his family had been caught in the cross-fire of several hunters.

To retaliate, Wakan returned to this ranch month after month, killing dozens of sheep on each visit.

Wakan approached the ranch early one spring. He noticed several buck sheep located in a high enclosure. Often he avoided attacking these male animals since they were usually aggressive and their horns were dangerously sharp.

Deliberately Wakan jumped over the high fence and circled the bucks. He continued to circle the animals, periodically darting toward one, then quickly moving back. After several minutes of this, the sheep became confused and began bumping into one another in an effort to keep their distance from the intruder.

Wakan took advantage of the commotion and began singling out individuals who turned their backs on him and were far enough away from the others so he could avoid being rammed.

He grabbed the hind legs of his victims, dragging them away from the others, then swiftly lunged at their throats and tore away at the jugular.

In less than an hour he slaughtered fifteen head of prize rams. Then, bored, he jumped back over the high fence and went to a resting place in the nearby hills.

Over a period of the next two weeks, Wakan returned to the enclosure and slaughtered the remaining twenty or so bucks in the herd. When he finished his grizzly task, nearly three dozen valuable sheep had been routinely killed.

Leaving the carcasses without eating anything, Wakan enraged the ranchers who owned the sheep.

The morning after he finished executing the prized animals, four riders began following Wakan's tracks. The lone wolf watched as the riders circled the sheep pen, then began pursuing his trail.

Wakan led the riders nearly forty miles the first day, making wide circles and continually staying just out of rifle range.

Watching the pursuers carefully, Wakan determined that three of the riders carried weapons while a fourth, the man riding the swiftest horse, did not carry a rifle.

When the riders spread out in an attempt to surround Wakan, he moved closer to the unarmed man and loped along in the tall grass a few hundred yards ahead of him.

Frustrated at not being able to shoot at the wolf, the man turned aside to notify the others he was close on the trail of "Three Toes".

When the rider quit following, Wakan turned down a small valley and disappeared into the heavy brush.

Lying quietly, resting in the tall growth, Wakan blended into the dried grass clumps. The riders returned to the area and searched for over an hour but did not discover the wolf. Wakan had chosen to end the chase.

The riders finally gave up and returned to their ranch.

Wakan stayed in the valley, resting after the ranchers left, then decided to move across the prairie, away from the sheep ranch.

In spite of all the destruction that man inflicted on Wakan and his family, the wolf still did not fear humans and often traveled close to their dwellings. He was curious about these strange creatures who were constantly chasing him.

Their attempts to trap him had not succeeded because they usually left their distinctive smell on everything they touched. Tempting pieces of meat or fat, laced with poison, were obvious to Wakan, although he noticed that coyotes regularly fell victim to both traps and poison.

Once, his meandering took him close to a town located a few miles away. He could see the buildings in the distance when he noticed a man watching him. The man excitedly rode into the town, shouting that he had spotted "Three Toes".

Within a few minutes, several people gathered in a pasture at the edge of the town. The wolf watched the humans as they began making plans to surround him.

Wakan moved away from the crowd, keeping an alert eye on them as they spread out to form a large circle. Soon they surrounded the section of land where he lay watching.

The wolf moved through the grass, crawling on his stomach to avoid being seen. He found a ditch with an overhanging ledge along a small washout. Cautiously, Wakan crawled under the overhang, completely hidden from view.

He lay quietly, listening for the sounds of the approaching people. After several minutes, he heard their voices fade away as they passed near his hiding place.

Slowly, Wakan eased out of his concealment and peeked over the edge of the washout. He could see riders moving away from him in the distance.

Still alert to danger, Wakan ran in the opposite direction, following the washout until he reached a level area. Once he reached a safe distance from the people searching for him, he cut across the prairie.

When he reached a dirt road, Wakan followed it, again heading toward the town. After he traveled a short distance, he spotted a woman riding alone on horseback.

Wakan scrutinized her carefully and determined that she had no rifle. He moved off to the side, a hundred yards or so from the woman, sat down and observed as she stopped her horse and looked at him.

After watching her for a few moments, Wakan turned and trotted slowly out of sight. When the woman moved on, Wakan followed her trail on the road until it reached the ranch where she was riding.

Wakan settled into the tall grass and waited until sunset. After darkness fell, the wolf slipped into the small horse pasture next to the corral on the ranch. There he discovered several head of horses. He selected the one he would exterminate.

The chase was deliberate and effective. Wakan circled the horses until he saw the one he had chosen, break away from the herd. He then stalked the horse, forcing it in a corner of the fence.

The animal panicked when it became trapped in the enclosure. Wakan darted back and forth, turning the horse into the fence each time it tried to escape. Finally, the horse broke for the center of the pasture. It was the opportunity Wakan waited for. He lunged at the rear leg of the horse, grabbing the animal and painfully tearing away the tendons and muscles.

The horse stumbled, giving Wakan the opportunity to sink his teeth into the horse's belly.

In pain, the horse tried to kick his attacker, but missed. Wakan held firm as the horse struggled to free itself.

Wakan lost his grasp momentarily, allowing the horse to regain its balance. The wolf moved to the other side and again attacked the fleeing animal. This time Wakan tore a huge hole in the horse's rear leg.

Patiently, Wakan allowed the horse to continue to run, staying a few feet behind the sharp hooves flying toward him.

Wakan persisted, waiting for the horse's wounded muscles to stiffen.

In a few minutes, the horse stopped, snorting as he turned to face Wakan. The wolf watched as the horse's wounds bled profusely.

Weakened by the mutilation of his rear quarters and the loss of blood, the animal began staggering away from the wolf. Wakan took advantage.

When the horse turned, Wakan again attacked from the side, leaping through the air, his razor sharp fangs tearing at the horse's throat.

With his windpipe slashed open, the horse fell to the ground. Wakan attacked the horse's mid-section, speeding his death.

Eating his fill, Wakan left the horse pasture and returned to the nearby hills. He spent the night in a small den overlooking the ranch where the killing had taken place.

At dawn, Wakan observed the rancher as he entered the horse pasture, finding the wolf's victim. The man began shouting, alerting other humans to the tragedy.

Quickly, they gathered the other horses into the corral, roped and saddled them.

The riders rode around the outside of the horse pasture until they found Wakan's distinctive three toed-tracks, then headed toward his hiding place.

Wakan stood up in full view of the riders. Each of them carried a rifle. One began shooting, but the others shouted at him to stop.

The wolf loped to the top of the hill and disappeared over the crest.

Throughout the day, the riders followed Wakan.

Wakan stayed out of sight as much as possible, yet the men continued to find his tracks.

Late in the day, Wakan observed that other riders joined the group. Now ten men were pursuing him.

About two hours later, two other riders with a pack of dogs arrived. The dogs took the lead, following Wakan's tracks.

Late in the afternoon, the dogs continued to gain on Wakan. They led his pursuers across the rough terrain near the Slim Buttes. Wakan crossed as many pasture fences as he could along the way.

The wolf had traveled every part of this territory. Over the years, he had memorized the landscape and knew how to escape.

Determined to lose the hunters and their dogs, Wakan entered a wide washout. The dogs' yapping was louder. They were closing in on him.

He followed the washout and came to an intersection where two other washouts converged with the one he had chosen. The washouts were divided by a twelve-foot gravel wall.

Wakan was leading the hounds by several yards when he stopped, leaped high into the air, and jumped completely over the wall, into the adjoining washout.

When the dogs reached the spot where Wakan jumped, they could find no sign of his scent. It was as if he had disappeared into thin air.

The hunters arrived on the scene and found the dogs milling around in circles, searching for a trail that no longer existed.

Wakan moved swiftly and within minutes he was safe, several miles away. Needing a rest, the wolf found a hiding place on the side of a large butte overlooking the valley below.

Wakan spent the night dozing, awakening periodically to sniff the air and reassure his safety.

The riders secured their dogs and returned to their homes. They had lost still another round against "Three Toes".

CHAPTER 25

Wakan's curiosity about humans was unexplainable. Even though he was often pursued by men, he still allowed himself to be seen during daylight hours.

Frequently he would sit on rock out-croppings, watching men build fences around their pastures. He spent hours scrutinizing humans as they worked with their cattle or sheep.

If the men became alert to Wakan's presence, he waited until they started coming after him before running away. He enjoyed these chases.

The ranchers were amazed at Wakan's great stamina. He could lope across country hour after hour without tiring.

Wakan learned that fences were his greatest ally when being pursued. He marked trails leading to pasture fences so that he could duck under the structures causing the hunters to stop and spend time taking down the wires to cross.

Wakan often took advantage of these delays to rest or to gain needed distance between himself and his trackers.

As Wakan got older, his tall sleek body became slimmer. He did not have to eat as often and found that weighing less was an advantage, especially when he traveled great distances.

During his years of taking revenge on the ranchers who murdered his family, Wakan often picked up companions.

Periodically, other lone wolves sought to follow him and he was even enticed sometimes by a lone female in heat. But he steadfastly refused to join with any other members of his species to form a pack.

Coyotes overcame their fear of the huge gray brute and followed him. They found splendid feasts in the wake of Wakan's massacre of farm animals.

The ranchers usually found several sets of tracks around cattle and sheep carcasses. Often there was one set of huge paw prints, one with the tell-tale three toes, and many smaller prints of coyote companions.

After traveling as a lone wolf for four years, Wakan had his second close encounter with man's vicious traps.

Following a wagon trail, Wakan was attracted to the scent of a female wolf on a sagebrush plant.

It had been months since he had seen any other wolves and his curiosity overcame his normal cautious approach. Sniffing around the plants, Wakan stepped onto an area of soft dirt with his right rear leg.

Immediately he felt the hard steel of a trap. He quickly jerked his leg away.

SNAP!

The trap caught the toes on Wakan's right rear foot.

Familiar pain shot up through his leg, Wakan pulled against the trap. Ignoring his pain, he kicked hard in an attempt to free himself from the steel teeth of the monster.

Remembering how he had suffered when he lost his front toes as a youngster, Wakan fought violently. Still the trap held.

For two hours the wolf thrashed and tugged against the trap. The jaws were firmly clamped behind the foot pads of two toes and had broken the bones.

Wakan lay down. He was exhausted from the pain and struggle. After contemplating his circumstances, the wolf began chewing on his foot just behind the vice-like trap jaws. His sharp fangs easily tore through the tough skin holding the two toes in the trap. In a moment he was free.

He lay quietly next to the trap, licking his wound and recovering from the shock. After about a half-hour, the bleeding stopped. Wakan slowly stood up to test his balance.

When he was rested and strong enough to continue on, Wakan moved sluggishly away from the trap, watching his every move in order to avoid other traps that were in the area.

It took Wakan nearly an hour to cover a mile. He limped up the side of a pointed hill and found a scattering of rocks near the top.

The wolf was relieved to find a resting place where he could allow the aching limb to recover. He stayed hidden in the rock enclosure for three days, licking his sore foot and allowing the stiffness to ease.

On the fourth night, Wakan left his seclusion in search of food. He hunted throughout the night but found he was unable to pursue his prey.

Wild game often proved too swift for the recovering wolf, but a nearby pasture provided an abundance of sheep. Wakan feasted periodically on an individual animal, eating the meat in order to regain his strength.

The injury to his rear foot curbed Wakan's activities for several weeks. He spent his days hidden among the rocks and tall grass of the buttes in the area. At night, he moved down into the valleys searching for food.

Wakan was cautious not to slaughter too many domestic animals, since he was afraid that would enrage the ranchers. He could not endure another chase until he recuperated.

After several weeks of recovery, Wakan left the area, making his way back to the western boundary of his territory.

Now, nearly healed and able to move normally, Wakan resumed his rampage against the livestock owners.

Wakan's popularity with his coyote cousins increased. A pack of a half dozen began to follow along behind him wherever he wandered.

At first, the wolf had little regard for these followers. Wakan did not trust coyotes and viewed them as foolish.

The coyotes were nearly always attracted to dead animals lying on the prairie. All too often they suffered strychnine poisoning or bit into sharp pieces of wood or metal encased in balls of animal fat lying around the carcasses.

Wakan did not eat meat from those carcasses. Experience taught him to be suspicious that man had placed poison in the flesh. Besides, Wakan did not need anyone to provide meat for him.

Wakan's compassion for these yellow canines increased and he often led the coyotes away from these temptations. On many occasions he provided fresh lambs or calves for the hungry followers.

The coyotes eventually served as watchdogs for the aloof wolf. They stayed near his lair when he slept and alerted him to any approaching danger.

The coyotes recurrently proved useful in hunting activities, surrounding deer and other wildlife, preventing them from escaping Wakan's attack.

Early one winter morning, Wakan crossed a pasture on his way to the area of his birth along the Little Missouri River. It had snowed lightly the night before and his tracks were obvious in the new-fallen snow.

Wakan outdistanced his coyote cousins as he made his way across the fenced-in meadow. He passed close to a log cabin occupied by two cowboys.

Shortly after he passed by, the ranch hands emerged from the cabin to feed their horses. One of the men noticed Wakan's tracks in the fresh snow.

Excited, the two men saddled their horses and rode toward the ranch headquarters.

Within an hour, they gathered all the hired hands and called on a neighbor to bring his tracking hounds.

Unknown to Wakan, more than a dozen men and a half-dozen dogs were on his trail.

Wakan first realized that he was being pursued when he heard the baying of the hounds. He ran to the top of a nearby hill and looked back across the prairie toward the sound.

He saw the riders and hounds following his tracks.

He immediately headed in the direction of the river. Wakan had a plan of escape.

The chase covered several miles. Wakan stayed well ahead of the hunters. After two hours, Wakan's rear leg began to ache. The wound had healed, but the muscles pulled and he found it awkward to run on the maimed foot.

Finally the river was in sight. Wakan searched for a familiar spot.

He moved rapidly toward a high bluff overlooking the winding river. He waited until the riders and dogs were within a half-mile.

Then, in plain sight of his pursuers, Wakan turned and jumped off the thirty foot embankment, landing in the soft river sand below.

Regaining his balance, Wakan ran into the heavy brush along the river bank. There he found a safe place to lie down and where he could observe the approach of the hunters and dogs on the bluff a few yards away.

Wakan watched as the dogs reached the edge of the cliff, barking and scurrying around looking for the wolf's scent.

The hunters dismounted near the edge of the cliff where they had seen Wakan jump.

Peering over the embankment, they were hoping to find the wolf's body lying in the river. They looked up and down the opposite river bank for sight of the cunning wolf. He was nowhere to be seen.

Frustrated and angry, they gathered their dogs, and put them on long leashes. Then they remounted their horses and rode away.

Wakan stayed in his hiding place, temporarily free of the threat of the hunters and their dogs. Here was able to rest his maimed rear leg.

CHAPTER 26

The battle between "Three Toes" and the ranchers raged for eight more years over a territory encompassing a thousand square miles.

His reputation grew with each of his attacks on livestock and with his miraculous escapes. Some applauded his courage and cleverness, but most hated him for his destruction and malicious killing of their livestock.

Yet he was admired for his tenacity.

Few understood why he persisted in this battle against overwhelming odds.

Wakan knew!

The last years of his life were dedicated to evening up the score between himself and those who tormented and killed the members of his species.

It was in Wakan's nineteenth year that his human equal came into the picture.

The man was known widely throughout the nation as one of the best wolf trappers around.

He had trapped hundreds of wolves in other parts of the country. He knew their habits, instincts, fears, knowledge and perceptions.

An early June thunderstorm, so common on the prairie, was raging when Wakan found shelter in a small cave in the Cave Hills.

He had just returned from the western part of his territory when the rain showers started. Lightning and rolling thunder urged the wolf into the rock-enclosed cavern.

Wakan had slaughtered a small deer early that morning and was spared from hunger then he settled down to rest. The weather was too nasty for hunters and the rain would wash away any tracks he may have left while crossing a creek in a nearby rancher's pasture.

The storm continued throughout the night, forcing Wakan to stay inside. In recent years, the chilly winds took their toll on the aging wolf, especially if he got wet and was without sanctuary from the elements.

Early the next morning, Wakan arose and sniffed the air to locate any enemies who might be traveling in the area. The air was fresh and clean, no danger was in sight.

He rested most of the day and started scouting the nearby ranch just before sunset. After amusing himself with a twig from a sage plant for several minutes, Wakan recalled how he learned to play while still a puppy.

Thoughts of Acayla came to his mind. He still missed his beloved mate and friend.

He missed his family and often wondered how they were surviving in their new territory.

Bored with the solitary game of playing catch, Wakan moved down the hill into a nearby creek-bed. The soft wet sand felt comfortable on his feet. He traveled along the creek for several yards before heading into a pasture.

The sun set and evening shadows cast their darkness at the base of the few trees along the bank.

Soon the moon would rise enabling Wakan to see as he performed his grizzly task of methodically eliminating as many of man's animals as possible.

He traveled throughout the night, moving from pasture to pasture, selecting a few unfortunate sheep along the way to be his victims.

Before morning light, Wakan found a resting place at the head of a small wash-out which was covered with last year's dry growth of grass.

Wakan was unaware that early that morning, two men were looking at his tracks in the soft creek sand where he crossed the night before.

"Those are Three Toes' prints," the rancher said to the wolfer.

The professional trapper took a wooden match from his pocket and measured the paw imprint.

"Seventy-five or eighty pounds," he announced.

"Seems like this wolf is bigger than that," the rancher argued.

"Nope. He has big feet, but doesn't weigh much," the trapper replied.

"For as much damage as he's done, I would have guessed that he was huge, maybe a hundred or a hundred-twenty pounds," the rancher added.

"It doesn't make any difference how big they are, it's how smart they are," the wolfer replied. "Let's follow these tracks, see if we can find out some of his habits."

Wakan spent the day resting. He slept well into the night, Shortly before midnight, he arose and found his way to a nearby pasture containing several young lambs and ewes.

Slowly and stealthily he moved into the enclosure, observing whether guard dogs or a sheep-herder were present. He circled the entire herd before starting his attack.

He walked quietly into the herd. A few ewes were disturbed by his presence, stamping their feet in annoyance.

With passive efficiency, Wakan grabbed the nearby lambs, crushing their small heads with his mouth. The old wolf had few teeth left to tear the skin, but his powerful jaws did the job just as well.

Within one half-hour, Wakan had killed three dozen lambs and piled them up next to a nearby water tank.

The ewes continued to bleat nervously, but were helpless to offer any resistance to the wolf. Then, bored with this activity, Wakan moved out of the herd and disappeared into the night.

The next morning, the rancher and the wolfer reviewed the carnage next to the water tank. The pasture and the tank were located within a half-mile of the rancher's home.

"I don't understand how he does it," the rancher exclaimed in anger. "He moves in like a shadow and quietly snuffs out three dozen sheep, and our dogs didn't even bark."

"I have an idea what we're dealing with here," the wolfer said. "We were so close to him, yet that doesn't seem to bother him at all. He's smarter than we imagined. I'd better get started setting some traps."

"It seems to me he's not afraid of people anymore," the rancher added, "and he knows where we are, what we're doing, and when there's danger."

The wolfer spent the day following tracks left by "Three Toes". He drew out a rough pattern and decided on the locations of a few more trap settings.

The man was meticulous about his settings, spending at least two hours on each one. He wore rubber gloves to keep the human scent off the traps which had been previously boiled in lye water to wash away all smell of oils left by human hands.

He carefully chose the sites of each trap, setting his main trap along the trail, then surrounding it with two or three others fixed to catch the wolf as he circled the main trap setting.

The rancher accompanied the wolfer while he performed his tasks.

"Look at that," the rancher remarked. "You can't even tell there's anything there."

"That's the way it needs to be," the wolfer responded. "Now let's see if we can fool "Old Three Toes" as easily," he laughed.

"How long do you think it'll take you to catch him?" the rancher inquired.

"I have a lot more traps to set and it'll take a few more days just to get set up right," the trapper said. "It all depends on luck."

"We could catch him tonight, but I'm counting on his getting careless and thinking we only have a few traps out," he added.

While the trap-setting activity continued, Wakan renewed his rounds of the neighborhood ranches. Each night he left his calling card in the form of slaughtered lambs and calves.

Each day the ranchers discovered his handiwork and grew more and more impatient.

Wakan began an orderly routine of checking the areas where the wolfer was working. He kept constant watch on these activities and periodically sprung the traps. The competition between wolfer and wolf became intense. Time would tell who would win.

Occasionally, during his nightly escapades, Wakan would find coyotes, badgers, skunks, and sometimes dogs caught in the traps. He often circled the ill-fated animal, letting the trapper know that he was not fooled by his handiwork.

He studied every trap setting trying to figure out how the wolfer plied his trade. He watched for patterns of how the trap was camouflaged. He used his keen sense of smell to determine which scents were being used.

Wakan instinctively recognized that the smell of the lye, used to remove human odor from traps, was not normally found in nature. Even this tactic became useless to the wolfer.

The trapper had taken great pains to complete each setting, but the cunning "Three Toes" had detected his method and continued to be an elusive target. "Three Toes" observed the configuration of the settings and repeatedly sprung the traps.

The professional had pinned his hopes on these settings but once he determined that "Three Toes" could not be captured by normally designed trap groupings, he decided to move to another location and try again.

"I guess we're dealing with a damned intelligent animal," the wolfer commented. He was speaking to several ranchers who had gathered to talk over the failure to capture "Three Toes".

"There's no doubt about his intelligence," one of them mused.

"He's been avoiding every kind of trap and poison for the last fifteen years," another voiced.

Still another observed, "If this would have been easy, we wouldn't have hired you to trap him."

"I think I've found a pattern to his movements," the trapper observed. "Tomorrow, I'm going to set some traps along a trail where I've found his tracks on several different occasions. If I get the traps set carefully enough, we might just get lucky and end this struggle."

The men knew by the tone of his voice that he too was bewildered and surprised at the tenacity of this wolf.

The professional wolfer re-visited the area where Three Toes frequented. It was on a ridge overlooking the Little Missouri River. He found an old trail that had not been lost by rain, but could find no sage brush on which to sprinkle the scent. He transplanted a few bushes to serve his purpose and set the traps he had prepared beneath the brush.

He placed five traps strategically around the sage brush. Each was located just far enough away from the bushes to catch a leg when the wolf stopped to smell the scent or mark the bush with urine.

He then left the setting, confident that this time he had found a satisfactory location. Hopefully it would be the last one he had to set up.

The traps remained undisturbed for ten days. Nothing happened.

Wakan had temporarily moved on to another part of the country, a few miles distant.

The trapper faithfully checked the more than two dozen settings he had placed for the ranchers in the area.

He traveled nearly fifty miles a day, resetting sprung traps and removing unfortunate game which had strayed too close.

No tracks with the tell-tale three toes were seen.

"I wonder if he's left the country," one of the ranchers remarked.

"Maybe, but I'll wager he'll be back," another added.

A third commented, "We might go for months and not see him, then again he could be back tomorrow. That's the way "Three Toes" operates."

Wakan had moved across the Montana border and was spending some time in a territory he had not visited in years. While the trap settings were being installed, he was nearly seventy miles away.

His reckless slaughter of farm animals continued. He delighted in making sure the owners knew who had been there. He made no secret of his presence wherever he traveled.

Over the next few days, Wakan killed animals in nearly every pasture he crossed. One of his victims was a yearling heifer he separated from the herd on the ranch where he had lost the toe on his right front paw.

He made a wide circle and arrived back at the area where the wolfer was tenaciously keeping watch over his traps.

Late on the mid-summer night of July 22, 1925, Wakan trotted along the banks of the river near the area of his birth.

His mind was on his family and on his youth. As he moved quietly along an old wagon trail, he thought again about his father Zando, his mother Laomi, and his love, Acayla.

He recalled the lessons they had taught him. Lessons about preserving heritage, about survival, about the significance of family, and about loyalty and strong relationships.

He thought about how different his life might have been, were it not for the hunters and trappers who had slain so many wolves.

Wakan knew that man's effort to exterminate his species, was implemented with total disregard for the order of *nature's spirit*, and that the life his ancestors lived would never be experienced again.

CHAPTER 27

Casually, Wakan noticed a sage bush along the trail. A slightly familiar scent was in the air, but he could not determine what it was.

Instinctively he stopped to smell the bush and mark his territory.

Suddenly his foot touched something strange. He started to pull back, then.....

SNAP!

The cold steel jaws of the trap clamped high on his right front leg.

Wildly Wakan pulled and twisted to escape.

He took a desperate lunge backward....

SNAP!

His left rear leg was clamped in the steel jaws of another trap.

He thrashed his body around, and dug at the ground with his free paws, biting, snarling, pulling and tossing his weight against each of his legs so painfully caught in man's merciless devices.

The wolf continued to struggle as the moon passed overhead and began to fade. The first light of dawn appeared on the horizon.

Finally, exhausted, he ended his battle and lay quietly with his head resting on his forepaws, waiting to meet his adversary.

His life was ending, and so was an era.

Wakan would be no more.

Man had finally caught "Three Toes".

He knew he was the last of the wolves to roam this territory.

He was the last to give up the struggle against the invasion of the white man and his domestic livestock.

He lay quietly, enduring the pain which was now subsiding as numbness engulfed both trapped legs.

Life was draining away.

He could think of nothing but relief and resignation.

When the wolfer arrived with his companions, Wakan looked at him with a cold, ceaseless stare.

His gray eyes showed no emotion.

The trapper lifted Wakan into the back of his vehicle. The wolf did not take his eyes off the man who succeeded in doing what over a hundred and fifty others had failed to do.

As his captor started the trip to the nearby town, life left Wakan's body.

But his unblinking stare continued.

It was over.

Now the white man would tell the story of the wolf who struggled against them and how they had won the victory over the last wolf.

But in spite of the human conquest of "Three Toes", Wakan and his ancestors will live on in the folklore of the plains Indians, and in the hearts of all who understand the wolf's special place in *nature's spirit*.

THE END

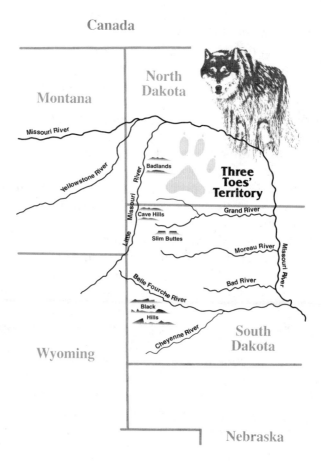